THE HUNTING GROUND

THE
HUNTING
GROUND

Cliff McNish

Orion
Children's Books

First published in Great Britain in 2011
by Orion Children's Books
a division of the Orion Publishing Group Ltd
Orion House
5 Upper St Martin's Lane
London WC2H 9EA

An Hachette UK Company

1 3 5 7 9 10 8 6 4 2

Text © Cliff McNish 2011

Library hardback ISBN   978 1 44400 192 1
Trade paperback ISBN   978 1 84255 993 2

Typeset by Input Data Services Ltd, Bridgwater, Somerset

Printed in Great Britain by CPI Mackays, Chatham, Kent

The Orion Publishing Group's policy is to use papers that are natural,
renewable and recyclable products and made from wood grown in sustainable
forests. The logging and manufacturing processes are expected to
conform to the environmental regulations of the country of origin.

www.orionbooks.co.uk

For Justina Robson, *optissima*

Contents

CONTENTS

I

THE VISITOR

Dead things can sound alive when they choose. Dead things can move around.

At first nothing woke sixteen-year-old Elliott. Asleep in bed, he failed to notice the eerie whispered rhymes. Or the sighs. Or the footsteps. Those footsteps came lightly and swiftly towards him – someone or something running incredibly fast across the floors of the old house. A presence long dead was on its return to the world of the living.

The visitor wrapped itself in its own hush. It pressed against cold walls, deeply excited. It swept its death inside shadows. It rarely came in a straight line. It came in impossible ways: soaring above lampshades, drifting between stuffed chairs. Passing over lush burgundy carpets, it never once needed to touch them. Floors are not only to be walked upon, one foot in front of another.

Gliding past portraits in the corridors, the visitor tenderly stroked them. It made time for that, kissing one or two of the less grimy paintings. Its lips, opening and closing upon the wooden frames, were never quite still.

To start with the visitor kept well away from the new occupants of Glebe House. Only when it was certain everyone was asleep did it travel from the East Wing to the first floor of the main house. Elliott's dad, Stephen, lay in his own room. He was turned away from the door, one of his bare arms inside the top blanket, the other flung across his pillow like an afterthought. The visitor knelt beside his face. For a while it simply stayed that way, gazing at his strong, muscular body.

Then it floated up to the third floor.

Elliott's fourteen-year-old brother, Ben, had his bedroom there. The visitor lurked just inside Ben's door, observing his chest rise and fall. It watched until the moon rose like a pale creamy promise in the window. Then it was drawn towards the partially-open bedroom opposite.

Elliott was inside, asleep on his back.

The visitor wafted smoothly up to his face. Its movements lightly stirred the air, sending up small puffs of dust. In gentle waves the dust settled on Elliott's black eyelashes, dotting the upturned tips grey. The visitor's mouth was an even deeper grey. Grey face, grey mouth. Lips pursed in the moonlight. Lips that never stopped murmuring. Tiny whispers. A rhyme that sparked the air, over and over.

'Where's the Ogre?
Where's he been?
Where's he hiding?
In your dreams . . . '

The visitor hovered over Elliott. It noted his strong chin, his slim, handsome face. He looked vaguely like someone the visitor had once known, and it had to resist an impulse to peel back his lids to check the colour of his eyes.

An hour passed. Maybe longer. It was hard to be sure. It had been a long time since time had meant anything much to the visitor.

Eventually, it left to collect something it had forgotten. When it returned, it was carrying a heavy object the size of a large baby. The visitor dragged the object's head across the wooden planks of the hallway. Dirty hair strands caught between scalp and floor made a harsh sliding *scrishhhh*.

And at last, hearing that extended sibilant hiss, Elliott woke.

2

GLEBE HOUSE

Lifting his face off his hard, scratchy pillow, Elliott peered around. He couldn't see anything wrong. No one was in the room. But he'd definitely heard a noise. It must have come from outside.

He sat up. He wasn't frightened yet. He'd been through so many house relocations that unusual noises didn't bother him. His dad was a renovator – paid to repair valuable old homes prior to resale. Every couple of years Elliott and his younger brother, Ben, were shunted off to another property, living there until Dad's work was finished. The new home they had moved into, an enormous mansion property called Glebe House, was just bigger than normal, that was all.

Scrishhhhh.

Intrigued now, Elliott sat up, wiping the tiredness out of his eyes. He'd learned to sleep peacefully through more or less anything: squirrels nesting in walls, infestations of mice, squawking birds. Glebe House, built mainly in the seventeenth century, had enough classic creaks and sighs to cause a little kid to wet the bed. Elliott and Ben always enjoyed tracking down those kinds of sounds in a new home. Especially the night-time ones. They were good at it.

Scrishhhhhhhh.

There it was again. And wasn't it closer to his room this time?

Twisting his head to and fro in the darkness, Elliott listened hard. Since arriving a couple of days ago, he and Ben had barely checked out a quarter of Glebe House. There were no less than twenty four bedrooms in the main building alone. Saying *Take your pick*, Dad had gestured for the boys to grab whichever ones took their fancy.

Elliott chose a room across the corridor from Ben on the third floor. They usually grabbed rooms close together if they could. Their mother had suffered a complicated breakdown when Ben was still a baby, and decided to leave the family. With all the house-swapping over the years, both boys forever coping with new schools, and Dad often busy, they'd come to rely on each other's company more than most brothers.

Scrishhh Scrish. Scri—

With alarm scattering like sparrows inside his chest, Elliott flung the sheets off his bed and stood tensely on the mattress, listening. Was an intruder in the house? The estate, empty for generations, was in the middle of the countryside, surrounded by fields. Maybe someone had secretly made a home for themselves here ...

Elliott checked the window overlooking the abandoned eastern part of the house. He was sure he'd just heard a sound from there. *Stay calm*, he told himself. *It's probably just animals.* But the next noise he heard exploded that possibility. Because when did an animal ever approach a bedroom sounding so *excited*? That's what Elliott heard now. Something with a mouth at the crack of his open door, panting.

'*Scrishhhhh ...*'

'Hey!' Elliott yelled to scare off whatever it was. At the same time he staggered into the hallway and bellowed at the top of his voice, 'Dad! Ben!'

A door opened from somewhere below him, and Elliott sighed with relief when he saw Dad stamping up the staircase in his dressing gown. 'Was that you making a noise just now?' Elliott asked him.

'No,' Dad said blearily. 'I was asleep. What noise?'

'Just a sec.' Elliott raced across the corridor to check his brother's room. Finding Ben in his usual coma-like sleep, he nudged him awake. 'Come on, get up,' he told him. 'Something's going on.'

Hastily gathering them all together in the corridor, he told them about the sounds.

'This had better be worth it,' Ben warned, yawning. 'What are we listening for? I can't hear anything.'

'Shush,' Elliott said. 'Stay quiet and you might.'

They waited for over a minute, but the scrishing noises had stopped. Glebe House sounded as empty as it was meant to be.

'I definitely heard something moving around,' Elliott said.

'People?' Dad gazed at him doubtfully.

'Not sure. It was a sort of sliding noise.'

'Sliding?' Ben said, deadpan. 'That sounds *really* scary.'

Elliott glared at him and turned back to Dad. 'I know how dumb it sounds, but there was something near my room. Then I heard another noise. It seemed to be coming from ... I think it might have been the East Wing.'

'The East Wing?' Dad repeated.

'Yeah. Why?' Elliott said, noticing the sharp glance Dad shot Ben.

The East Wing was Glebe House's great mystery – the one part of the property still boarded up. Dad's first instruction to the boys had been to keep well away from it because it was unsafe. From the evasive look now on Ben's face, Elliott could tell that he'd ignored the order.

'Your brother was up late exploring in there,' Dad told Elliott, clearly annoyed. 'At least he got his reward.'

'What reward?'

Dad motioned, and Elliott saw a bump on the left

side of Ben's head. The swelling wasn't large, but it was surrounded by a nasty, discoloured bruise.

'It's nothing to do with the East Wing,' Ben said quickly. 'I did it on the way to the kitchen. I was hungry. But none of the lights work, so I missed a step, fell over, that's all.'

Elliott had an impulse to laugh in Ben's face, he was so obviously lying. He held back, partly because they automatically tended to back each other up, but also out of sheer surprise. If they were going to take risks like this, they mostly did it together. It wasn't unusual for Ben to sneak into some crumbling part of a house he'd been warned about, but why hadn't he got them both involved if he was so interested in checking out the East Wing?

They stayed listening for a while longer, but the house remained silent, and finally Ben headed back to his room.

'What were you doing in the East Wing?' Elliott mouthed silently over Dad's shoulder, but Ben ignored the question, firmly shutting his door. Elliott wondered what was going on. Secretive behaviour wasn't Ben's style at all. The nervous, distracted glance he'd given Elliott before closing the door hadn't been like him either.

'He definitely went into the East Wing tonight,' Dad said, once they were away from Ben's room. 'What

I don't understand is why he's denying it.'

'He probably thinks you'll punish him.'

'I told him I wouldn't. Still couldn't get a word out of him.'

'Why don't you believe his story about falling down the stairs?'

'Because he came into my room last night with his feet covered in East Wing dust, that's why,' Dad said. 'A little grey trail of it led right back there. I found the main entrance prised open. Ben denies it, but I didn't break the barrier down. Unless you ...'

'No way,' Elliott said.

'OK, that's what I thought. But Ben ... well, I guess curiosity got the better of him.'

Elliott frowned. 'You say he came to your room?'

'Yeah, and he was upset, too. Hiding tears. As soon as he saw me he recovered his nerve, but something strange must have happened to him in that place because he was all emotional. At first I thought it might be his head injury, but that's just superficial. Whatever happened to him in there, though, he doesn't want to talk about it.'

'You reckon he got lost inside?'

'Probably. There's no working electricity in that part of the house. He could easily have slipped and hit something. Scared himself. Only ...' Dad hesitated ' ... I've been trying to work out how he got in there.

Whoever originally sealed the East Wing up used a cross-pattern of reinforced wood bracing. That's pretty hard to shift.'

'You don't think Ben could have opened it?'

'No, he could have done it. It's just that it would have taken him ages. He must have been standing there for hours in the dark, patiently dismantling the wooden slats layer by layer. And he took it down quietly as well, or I'd definitely have heard something.' Dad shrugged, gave Elliott a tired grin. 'Oh, well, I'll ask him again tomorrow. Or more likely he'll tell *you* what happened.'

'Yeah, you know Ben,' Elliott said lightly. 'He can't keep anything to himself for long.'

But secretly Elliott was more concerned than he was letting on. If there was anything Ben hated it was big shows of emotion. It would have taken a lot to drive him into Dad's room. Why didn't he just come and tell me what happened? Elliott wondered.

Dad yawned and clapped an arm around Elliott's shoulder. 'Before we go back to bed, let's make sure we haven't got an unwanted guest sharing the house with us, eh?'

Elliott nodded, grateful to have Dad taking him seriously as they searched the house. For over an hour they went methodically from room to room, finding nothing. They ended up at the attic on the fifth floor. Easing out a stiff set of iron steps latched to the ceiling,

Dad made his way up and squeezed through the narrow entranceway. He shone a torch around.

'Well, well, no intruders,' Dad chuckled, 'but some poor girl's missing out.'

'What's up there?'

'A doll's house. Looks like a vintage model, too. Someone loved it enough to preserve it in mint condition. You want to see it?'

'Nope,' Elliott said dryly.

After the search was over Elliott said goodnight to Dad and went back to his own bedroom. He hadn't quite decided to dismiss the noises, though, and lay awake for a long time. He was just beginning to nod off again when he had a feeling that someone was inside the room with him.

Quickly sitting up, he stared around. No one was there, but for a moment he thought he heard the lilting echo of a rhyme. Then he wondered if it was his own breath scaring him. What was going on? It wasn't like him to be this jittery. He always settled fast into a new place. Why was he so jumpy?

Glancing around his musty bedroom, Elliott shivered. The furnishings had been untouched for decades and, as he peered up at the ceiling, a feeling crept over him. It was a feeling of being indescribably *alone*. Not scared – at least not scared enough to wake Dad or Ben up again –

but horribly lonely. Elliott wasn't sure why. It wasn't a feeling he associated with himself. He didn't know where it came from.

Propping himself up on his elbow, he checked the room again. His bed creaked and it was cold. Despite being the middle of summer, after years of neglect and lack of heating the entire house felt clammy and abandoned. There wasn't even an aerial for TV or an internet connection in Glebe House, and in the dreary silence Elliott missed his friends. They'd moved over a hundred miles from the last house, so seeing them wasn't going to happen anytime soon. All their lives Dad had taken on generally less interesting or well-paid work so that Elliott and Ben could at least attend the same schools across whole academic years, but money was tight at the moment and the Glebe House contract had simply been too lucrative to turn down.

Elliott sighed. Until he started his A-levels at his new college in a month's time, the chances of bumping into any interesting company were thin. Glebe House was so isolated that it took a full ten minutes to walk from the iron-grilled front gates to the main house. The grounds were endless as well. But Elliott had already decided that getting to know new people could wait. He'd make plenty of new friends in college in September. He and Ben would be outsiders here for a while, of course, but they were used to that, and could rely on each other.

Yawning, he reached for his MP3 and played a few random tracks. Half an hour later, still feeling restless, he decided to get up. He'd check the house again. Do it on his own this time, without Dad holding his hand. A point of pride.

Striding through the bedroom door, he paced to the end of the corridor.

A wide staircase curved below him. The staircase was oak-panelled and swept down to a cavernous hall. The hall was the centrepiece of the house. Dad had told Elliott that its white-mottled marble floor alone was worth more than the entire last house he'd done up.

Elliott didn't care. He preferred carpets.

Looking down, he could see the entrance to the high-ceilinged morning-room. Two broad reception rooms lay beyond that, which overlooked a sizeable lake. Glebe House even had its own library. When they were built the rooms must have been light and airy, but now they were mostly shuttered and obscured by dirt.

Elliott paused at the top of the staircase. Without admitting it to anyone, he'd been unnerved by his first sight of Glebe House. The property, unusually for a seventeenth-century dwelling, was five storeys high, and set at all sorts of crazy angles. Trees had been left to grow unchecked as well, so that they now shaded two-thirds of the house for most of the day.

But perhaps the most sinister aspect was the paintings. The main house was filled with oil portraits of its first owner. The man had placed literally hundreds of portraits of himself in every room, corridor, alcove and stairwell of the property.

In each portrait the owner was dressed in leather outdoor clothing – hunting attire – and stood with a weapon in his hand. Sometimes the weapon was a gun. Other times a sword. The owner had obviously favoured knives, but occasionally his weapon of choice was something more exotic, like a musket, crossbow or lance. And in all the portraits, lying at his feet, was the animal he had just killed. A fallow deer, its throat coated in blood. A hairy-sided boar. Doves. Gutted fish. White-feathered owls. Other birds, too, their lifeless feathers always spread wide by the owner's own hand.

There were even cats and dogs. Elliott had paused for a long time to look at the owner's expression when he saw those. There was almost a smile there. It was as if on that particular day he'd run out of wild things on the estate to kill, so rather than wait had simply chosen one of his loyal hunting hounds or even a pet to terrorise.

The owner was always the central figure in the portraits. He was a tall, broad-shouldered man with a tight, red-curled beard, small close-set eyes and fleshy lips. The teeth protruding from those lips were large and exceptionally white. Maybe the owner had asked the artist to touch up their whiteness to improve his looks, but Elliott didn't think so. Otherwise, surely he'd also have asked for the goofyness the oversized teeth gave him to be smoothed out as well. The owner's expression in the paintings was always enigmatic, too. It was as if even after all this time dead he still held the advantage, knew something you did not.

But the portraits weren't the only ominous aspect of Glebe House. The estate had its own graveyard as well, hunkering in cold stone next to a church at the northern edge of the grounds. Locals from the village a mile or so away had used it for centuries to bury their dead.

And then there was the mysterious East Wing.

What had happened to Ben inside there? He'd find out tomorrow.

Stretching out his arms, Elliott checked the time: nearly two a.m. No wonder he was so tired. Giving the third-floor corridor a last quick once-over, he returned to his room, slid back under the bed covers and tucked the musty blankets around his shoulders.

Then he listened. Glebe House was settling down for the night, its timbers and ironwork contracting with the cold. Elliott smiled as he heard the ancient mattress on his bed groan under his weight. Gradually, to that familiar, unfrightening sound, he drifted off to sleep.

But just before he did so he realised that he could hear a distant noise again. It was like a voice whispering incessantly. But the sound was faint, and Elliott dozed off with its puzzle still trickling across his mind.

*

Once Elliott was fully asleep, the grey-faced visitor made its way back inside his bedroom. It flashed rapidly through his doorway this time. The hours were beginning to speed up for it again.

Elliott lay on his back with his mouth open. In the moonlight his tongue glistened like a wet shining disk. Keeping to the shadows, the visitor watched that tongue closely. It opened its own smaller mouth, imitating his expression.

Then it retreated again. Fetching the baby-sized object up from the floor, the visitor kissed it once, twice, before dragging it away back down the staircase. And as it departed, it sang a little ditty:

> Five minutes to midnight,
> Five minutes to treason,
> Here comes the truth without the reason.
> No time left for fathers & children,
> Here comes the ogre,
> Into his season.

3

THE OLD WOMAN

Next morning over breakfast Elliott noticed that Ben was back to his usual cocky, confident self. There was none of the subdued irritability of last night. His hazel-green eyes twinkled when Dad mentioned the doll's house.

'Did you play with all the dolls inside, then?' he asked Elliott.

'I gave each of them a good hour,' Elliott replied. 'I knew they'd get grumpy otherwise.'

Ben leaned forward. 'I bet you loved it.'

'Don't worry,' Elliott said. 'I left them all out for you. You can sneak up there when we're not around.'

Dad reached for the milk. ''Course,' he said airily to Elliott, 'I still remember you playing with my old train set when you were Ben's age.'

'I was *nine* when I stopped playing with that, actually,' Elliott pointed out, which made Dad and Ben both roar with laughter.

Towards the end of breakfast, Elliott gazed out

17

through the kitchen's double-bay windows at the western gardens. A huge area of tiered lawns, collapsed walls and dried-up ornamental fountains met his eye.

'You've really got your work cut out this time,' he said to Dad.

'You're not kidding,' Dad groaned. 'The garden features alone will take another week. I've even been asked to hose down the gnomes.'

'The gnomes?'

'Trust me, they're out there. The grass is so long the little fellas are hiding.'

Ben looked up from his plate. 'Dad?' he said hesitantly. 'When you got given this job, were you told anything about the house?'

Both Dad and Elliott turned in curiosity towards Ben. He normally didn't care about the history of a property.

'Why do you ask?' Dad said.

'No reason. It's just ... the portraits.' Ben stared self-consciously around him. 'They're weird, aren't they? But sort of interesting as well. Do you know anything about him? The man in the pictures, I mean?'

'Not really,' Dad said, rubbing his stubbled chin. 'But you only have to look at the paintings to know there was something wrong with him. All those animals he was so proud of killing. Plus, well, I've never come across anything like the East Wing before.'

'It's not a standard build, is it?' Elliott said.

'No,' Dad answered. 'It's a bespoke job. A truly nasty bit of construction. Now that it's been conveniently opened up' – Dad didn't avoid looking at Ben – 'I've had a chance to check around in there. It's a labyrinth. Deliberately underlit and confusing throughout. Literally hundreds of criss-crossing corridors that all lead back on themselves.'

Ben stared down at the table and, glancing at him, Elliott thought, *You really did get lost in there, didn't you.*

'From the outside the East Wing looks innocent enough,' Dad said. 'Inside's another story. It's full of nearly identical rooms. One half is all bedrooms, the other half all bathrooms. And the longer corridors look as if they run in a straight line, but don't. They bring you in a circle, only so gradually that you can't tell. I used a compass to navigate, and I still nearly got lost inside there.' Dad chewed his lip. 'I did a bit of research on it before we got here, actually. The East Wing wasn't part of the original property. The seventeenth century owner who appears in all the portraits constructed it about ten years after he built the rest of the estate. He also seems to have had a raw love of the hunt. The East Wing's full of his vicious portraits.'

Ben kept his face lowered, but he was listening closely to Dad.

'I didn't know there were portraits in the East Wing as well,' Elliott said.

'More if anything.' Dad pulled a sour face. 'And it's not only birds and animals he's hunting in there, either. I'm not sure what fantasies he was entertaining when he had the paintings done, but they're not canvases you or I would hang on a wall. If you ask me, that whole part of the house should have been bulldozed into the hillside centuries ago. Pulled down and sent up in smoke.'

Elliott blinked in surprise. He'd never heard Dad react so strongly against a property. The owners, occasionally, but never the buildings themselves.

'It was an odd commission, actually,' Dad admitted. 'The whole estate's been lying idle, boarded up for a couple of generations.'

'They just left it like this?' Elliott asked.

'Reading between the lines there was some kind of tragedy here,' Dad said. 'Whatever happened, the latest owners didn't want anything more to do with the house afterwards. Even now they just want to sell it as fast as possible, get it off their hands. It's such a waste. There are genuine antiques all over this estate that have just been left to rot. I suppose the current owners have their reasons for abandoning it this way but, well, anyhow, it's half a century since it was last used as a home.' He stared thoughtfully out over the gardens. '*Something* happened here. I just don't know what.'

'Could have been illness in the house, I suppose,' Elliott suggested.

'Or somebody died,' Ben murmured.

Dad and Elliott both turned towards him.

'What makes you say that?' Dad asked.

Ben shrugged. 'Dunno. But it's possible, isn't it?'

*

After breakfast, Elliott decided that he'd been patient enough. It was time to take Ben for a walk in their giant new garden and find out what had happened last night.

'Come on. Shoes. Now,' he said, from the door of Ben's bedroom.

'I'm not going out,' Ben announced. 'No chance.'

'No chance, eh?'

A bit of mindless pestering later, Elliott had Ben reaching for his trainers.

'All right, but I'm not talking about it,' Ben growled, 'and I'm not going out for long.'

'Ten minutes.'

'Ten minutes max.'

They walked side by side through the vast oak front doors of the house and out into vivid morning sunshine. Elliott was guiding Ben southwards, towards the open pit where the lake used to be, when he spotted the woman.

She looked to be around sixty-five years old. Slim, with white, shoulder-length hair, she was on the other side of the perimeter fence, heading away from them, but Elliott felt a flutter in his stomach when he saw her dress. It was covered in flowers. Not printed flowers, but real ones. Dozens were pinned to the dress's pleats and folds: daisies, peonies, chrysanthemums, roses. Some were fresh. Others, more disturbingly, were withered, their petals dried or fallen out altogether. The woman's face was in profile, so he couldn't properly see what she looked like at first. But then she turned to gaze at them.

Elliott was drawn straight to her eyes. Even from this distance he could see that they were strikingly twilight-blue.

For several seconds the woman held each of the boys in an unsettlingly sharp regard. Then she acknowledged them with a curt nod of her bird-thin neck, smelled one of the fresher roses near her collar and stepped smartly on towards the graveyard at the edge of the estate.

'Who was *that*?' Elliott wondered, once she'd gone.

Ben shrugged. 'Must be one of the crazy locals,' he said, crossing his eyes.

They walked further into the grounds. To their left, the jutting East Wing spread across the lawns like an unsightly growth. It was by far the largest structure on the estate – a vast, hexagonal-shaped building three times the area of the main house. Elliott didn't like it. To him its irregular blank walls looked as if they had been erected with maximum ugliness in mind.

Ben didn't once look towards the building. Instead he headed steadfastly away from it, listlessly kicking sods of grass.

'So what happened, then?' Elliott asked at last. 'Look, if you need me to keep it secret from Dad, I will. You know that. Just tell me what went on in there.'

'You promise you won't say anything to Dad?'

'I promise.'

Elliott waited expectantly, but Ben fell silent again. No, it was more than silence. He looked upset, couldn't get his words out. Elliott had never seen Ben look so vulnerable before, and instinctively he stood a little closer to him. What was going on? If he was in trouble, Ben was normally willing to talk to Elliott even if he didn't talk to anyone else. Not this time.

Elliott tried to lighten the mood with a few jokes, but it made no difference. Ben was wound up tight. And there was a strange touch of hurt in his eyes as well. Seeing it disturbed Elliott even more than the bursts of irritation he sensed simmering in Ben just under the surface. What on earth had happened to him in the East Wing's corridors?

'You're acting a bit freaky, you know,' Elliott said.

'Nah, I'm all right,' Ben said. 'Just tired, that's all. Didn't sleep much.' He stopped and gazed back the way they'd come. 'But I hate this house, don't you?'

Elliott didn't have any strong feelings about the

property yet, but he played along, nodding agreement.

They were standing by the drained lake now. It was enormous, covering a full quarter of the estate. Twenty feet below their feet wet mud caked the bottom.

'I wonder why it's empty?' Ben said – the first sign of curiosity he'd shown since entering the garden.

'The lake's empty, and no one around for miles,' Elliott muttered.

'No one around for miles and nowhere to go,' Ben echoed. 'So what are we going to do?'

They both yelled together, *'Jack all!'*

It was a standard joke between them whenever they came to a new house.

Ben gingerly felt his bruise. 'You can stop following me round, you know, Elliott,' he said. 'I'm OK.'

'If you say so,' Elliott answered, seeing that Ben looked anything but OK. 'But if it's that interesting in the East Wing, I want to know what's inside.'

Ben firmly shook his head. 'You don't want to go in there, Elliott.'

'No? Why's that, then?'

Ben stared at his shins. He wouldn't meet Elliott's eye. 'Look,' he murmured, taking an uncertain breath. 'I don't want to talk about it. I don't even know why I went into the East Wing last night, OK? I know it was stupid. I woke up and I was looking at one of the portraits. Next I knew I was downstairs outside the East

Wing. I'm not even sure how I got in there.'

Elliott gave Ben space to say more. He didn't.

'Actually ... I think I heard the same noise as you last night,' Ben admitted, changing the subject. 'Before I went to sleep, I mean. *Scrishing* – is that what you called it?'

Elliott nodded. 'Yeah. What do you reckon it was? We can usually figure these things out.'

Ben scratched his chin. 'A rat, maybe?'

'Pretty big rat.'

'Something else then. Could have been a lot of things, I suppose.'

'Yeah, it could have been. But we're alone in the house, aren't we? Or supposed to be. What does that tell you?'

Ben shrugged.

'It's obvious, isn't it?' Elliott folded his arms. 'You heard the sounds as well. Something made them. Me and Dad went round with a torch checking every room last night and found them empty.'

Ben grinned, realizing what Elliott was suggesting, and also realizing that Elliott didn't believe it for a second.

'It's a ghost!' Ben cried, sending crows scattering from a nearby tree.

They both laughed aloud, and for a few seconds all the tension was broken.

'Whoo-whoo!' Ben said sarcastically. 'Don't wake them up. They're probably all over the garden.'

'Maybe,' Elliott said, enjoying himself as well now. 'Or is it just one person?'

'A single ghost, you mean? Someone who died here? Yeah.' Ben smiled. 'Someone who died horribly. So now they're out for revenge.'

'Yep,' Elliott agreed. 'And the ghost's going to be especially hacked off as well, because it's had to wait all this time to get it.'

'So you don't think we're gonna be OK?'

'No chance.'

'Not even if there are two of us against one ghost?'

'But there won't be two of us, will there?' Elliott said with a grin.

'Why's that?'

'Because I'm not sticking around to help you. As soon as I see a ghost I'm off.'

'Thanks,' Ben muttered. 'Don't expect me to save you when the ghost comes looking for you, then. C'mon,' he yelled. 'I'll race you back to the house.'

4

THE DIARY OF
THEO STARK

When they got back Ben headed straight upstairs while Elliott went to look for something to eat. He was concentrating so hard on finishing off a mustard-smeared ham sandwich as he left the kitchen that he clattered into Dad coming out of the hall.

'Sorry,' Dad chuckled, seeing Elliott jump. 'This place is making us all a bit jittery, eh? I thought you might like to have a look at these.' He held out some loose sheets of paper.

Elliott took them from him. 'What are they?'

'A diary. The beginning of one, anyhow. I found it when I was clearing the library. Weird I didn't find it earlier, actually, since I've been in there most of the morning. It was just lying on a chair for anyone to see. There are only six or seven pages, but if a tragedy did occur here a couple of generations ago, the diary date is about right. Which is curious, isn't it?'

Elliott looked at the top sheet. It was a title page,

handwritten in blue faded ink. In bold, underlined letters the cover proclaimed:

The Diary of Theo Stark

The paper was lined, discoloured around the edges and dry to touch. It had clearly been waiting a long time to be discovered. Dad glanced at Elliott, obviously interested in what he thought.

'Neat writing,' Elliott said, knowing it was a stupid remark under the circumstances, but unable to think of anything else to say.

'Schools taught people to write with formal correctness in those days,' Dad told him. 'It's the diary of a teenage boy. I've only had a quick look at it, but it's entertaining.'

'Yeah?'

Elliott turned to page one.

Hello! I'm Theo, and this, dear friend, is the premier entry in my first ever diary – a vaguely exciting moment for me anyway.

Don't ask me why I've decided to start a diary. There's just something about this weird house that makes it seem worth it. My little sister, Eve, says diaries are dumb, but she's only seven and classifies everything not related to herself or her

dolls as dumb, so we'll ignore her view about everything.

OK. Date and time check. It's 9.42 a.m. on, let's see, the 13th September 1962. OK, a few facts. I'm sixteen, brown hair, six feet tall, well, only three inches less than that, and—

Hold on. Mum just looked over my shoulder and says I'm starting all wrong. She says you're supposed to *confess* things in diaries. That's what they're for, she reckons. So, since she's being so nosy, I think I'll start off by confessing something on her behalf. Her hair caught fire yesterday. Interesting to watch, actually. She was bending over a candlelit table on Dad's birthday, about to kiss him, when she got a bit too close to the flame. What I learned in that moment is that *you absolutely cannot control how fast hair burns*. Mum was all right, but Dad missed out on his kiss.

Right, I'm starting to ramble already. Mum's an artist and she says because I take after her that's inevitable – the rambling, that is.

By the way, she recreated the singeing moment this morning over breakfast. She used hay strands and leftover bits of bacon rind to symbolise her hair before setting it alight. Typical of Mum. I'm used to her wacky ways, but I tend to keep her away from my friends. Actually, what am I talking about? I haven't got any friends here. Glebe House's latest owners are on some kind of extended holiday in Italy or something, so Mum, who knows them, nagged/begged Dad to grab the house for the year while they're away. So here we are – middle of nowhere. I haven't even got much to do. I finished school in July, and still haven't decided what to do yet.

Anyway, now you know my family. We've been in Glebe House for about a week already. It's weird here. There are these strange portraits everywhere, and the place is so big. You never know where anyone is.

Elliott lowered the pages. 'Have you read the rest?' he asked.

'No,' Dad said. 'Only the start. Like I said, there's not much. Only a handful of pages. Pity, really. He sounds like an interesting boy.'

Elliott nodded. Rifling through the sheets, he checked back to the date. September 1962. So the diary must have been written shortly before the house was boarded up.

'Hang on to it,' Dad said. 'I'm repairing woodwork in the library. If I find any more pages I'll let you know. And Elliott' – he eyed him seriously – 'I don't want you or Ben going anywhere near the East Wing. Stay safe, eh?'

'You bet.'

Elliott casually read a few more lines of Theo's diary, then took it upstairs with him. Would Ben be interested? Probably not. He tended to dismiss anything old. But Elliott decided he might as well show it to him.

When he got to Ben's room, however, it was empty. Checking around, Elliott finally found him on the second floor landing. At first, Elliott thought that Ben was just staring at a blank wall. Then he realised that his gaze was fixed on one of the portraits of the owner.

'What are you doing?' Elliott asked.

'I'm looking at this picture, that's what I'm doing,' Ben said, folding his arms. 'I can't work it out. It's not like the other portraits.'

Glancing up, Elliott saw that Ben was right. Instead of the usual figure of the owner grinning cheesily over his kill, this painting showed only a single arm.

'It's definitely still the original owner,' Ben said.

'How do you know?'

'I recognise the brown leather hunting cuff on his wrist.'

Impressed, Elliott looked again. The arm was skilfully constructed to guide your eyes down towards the bottom of the canvas. That's where the hand was – in the act of throwing something. The palm was open, fingers splayed wide. The owner looked as if he had just cast a weapon towards the viewer. Perhaps a throwing knife.

The hand was so lifelike and realistically proportioned that Elliott instinctively turned round to look for the weapon, as if it might be behind him.

The picture unnerved him. In the other portraits the owner's weapons were always on clear display. In this painting it was as if the owner was hiding something – or as if he did not want to reveal his full intentions just yet. With a jolt, Elliott realised, *He's playing games with us. The toothy old owner has been dead all these years, but he's still having his bit of fun.*

Elliott couldn't help smiling at that: the sheer audacity of the owner trying to wriggle his way inside people's heads after all these centuries. But he didn't like the way Ben kept staring at the picture.

'C'mon, let's go,' he said to him. 'Dad's found something worth checking out.'

Back inside Elliott's room, Ben surprised him by grabbing the diary pages, instantly curious. 'What are we waiting for?' he said eagerly. 'Let's read it.'

Elliott let Ben catch up with Theo's introduction, then they flipped through a handful of pages that were mostly descriptions of the nearest village. Part-way down the next section, though, Elliott came across this:

5th October. Hi again. Eve just did an amazing thing. She went out with one of Mum's art pads and came back with a really impressive sketch of

trees near a slope. Mum and Dad are both in awe. Until now Eve's just been proudly handing us stick-type drawings. None of us know where this great new leap in skill's come from. Mum's jumping for joy, of course. Even more so when Dad had the idea of getting Eve to sketch her favourite doll, Katerina.

Eve got all bashful and went off on her own to do the sketch – for some reason she's been hiding herself away a lot recently. But the picture she brought back was ... well, the likeness is nearly perfect.

Katerina's not the prettiest doll in the world. She's not pretty at all, in fact. She's just a humungous hard plastic *baby-thing* with loads of blonde hair that Eve never stops combing. Eve got her as a present from Nana Bertha ages ago, and she's been carting her round ever since. This is the first year Eve's been strong enough to carry her with one hand. I wish she'd still use two hands, though. Eve drags her everywhere by her feet. All we hear all day long is Katerina's hair sliding across the floorboards.

Ben looked up wide-eyed from the diary.

Elliott also raised more than an eyebrow. 'Are you thinking what I'm thinking?'

Ben nodded numbly, then laughed. 'But it can't be, can it? You think a doll's hair was making that noise?'

'I hope not,' Elliott said seriously.

They both bent closer to the diary.

10th October. I met a girl a few days ago. Her name's Janey Roberts. Her family live in a tiny little detached house just outside the estate. She's a year or two older than me, and she's tall, with these really intense blue eyes and straight black hair.

Eve started calling it *witch-hair* as soon as she saw her. That's dumb. Janey's hair isn't witchy at all, but for some reason Eve's taken an immediate dislike to her. If you need any proof of that you only have to look at the horror sketch Eve did. It made Janey look like a monster. For the record, Janey doesn't look a bit like a monster. She's quite pretty, actually. She was home schooled. Seems to have a lot of time on her hands as well, because she's forever wandering on her own around the Glebe estate.

Eve won't explain why she drew such a nasty sketch of Janey. I didn't even know she *could* draw a sketch as freaky as that. Mum's been telling everyone about how brilliant Eve is, but she was upset when she saw the Janey picture. Eve didn't care, though. She just added the flowers and left the sketch with us.

Actually, I wonder if it was the flowers which freaked Eve out so much. Janey always wears a dress with real flowers on it. Not that bizarre, you might think, but at any one time about a third of the flowers are shrunken and dead. I asked Janey why she doesn't get rid of the dead ones. She told me that she wears them '*as long as she can, even if they're not in season, because they're the children's favourites. The children choose them*'.

I've no idea what she's on about. It's typical of Janey to talk in riddles like that. She's a loner. She never seeks my company out or anyone else's. She's kind of intriguing, to be honest.

14th October. Eve keeps mysteriously disappearing. It's not so much the way she goes off on her own without any explanation that's worrying. It's that we keep finding her standing in front of the old owner's portraits. I spotted her twice today doing it. Looking at a dead guy and his slaughtered animals. I don't get it. Little kids can be funny sometimes, can't they?

Elliott glanced sidelong at Ben to see if he was getting the parallel. He didn't seem to be.

'What?' he said, impatient to continue.

'Never mind,' Elliott answered, turning back to the diary.

35

16th October. Janey walks around in flimsy dresses all the time. That's OK in summer but it's getting colder now. Worried about it, Mum and Dad decided to introduce themselves to Janey's parents. Mum looked like she'd been crying when they got back. 'They weren't very welcoming,' was all Dad said at the time. But later Mum told me that Janey's house is a filthy tip. 'They're allowing that girl to rot freely in a dark, private universe all of their own making,' she said angrily.

Whatever Mum meant by that, since then she's given Janey free run of the estate. She can go where she wants. Janey's invited in for meals, too, which she always eats fast and without stopping. You can see how hungry she is sometimes. Mum and Dad have both taken a real liking to her. Janey won't talk about her home life to us, but I can already tell whose parents she'd rather have.

5
SEVERAL SHADES
OF BLUE

Elliott lowered the page. He thought about the old woman they'd seen walking past the grounds. The diary was fifty-odd years old, so she was about the right age to be Janey.

'C'mon,' Ben said restlessly. 'Keep reading. There's not much left.'

18th October. The way Eve keeps hanging around the owner's portraits is weird enough, but now she's started creeping inside the East Wing as well. Why anyone would want to go near that place I've no idea. Oddly, though, I think it frightens her. I caught her crying in there today, near the entrance. 'Scared, scared,' was all she'd say, unable to take her eyes off one of the portraits inside.

Eve wouldn't say what had scared her so much, but she wouldn't leave either. I had to practically drag her out in the end. As soon as we were back in the hall her arms went around my knees, holding

on tight. Looking at her, I don't think Eve even knows what she's scared of. Mum can't get any sense out of her, either. She's already told Eve off about going into the East Wing. Dad's going to make sure it doesn't happen again by blocking off the entrance.

Elliott stopped reading. Outside, mid-morning sunshine shone in bursts through the bedroom window, lighting up the bruise on Ben's head.

'Hey,' Elliott said, prodding him. 'You paying attention to this?'

'Yeah.'

'So?'

'So what?' Ben demanded.

'So you're doing the same thing, that's what,' Elliott said bluntly. 'You're going into the East Wing just like Eve did.'

Ben gave Elliott a puzzled look. 'What do you mean?'

'You know what I mean.'

'But I only went in there once,' Ben protested. 'It's not the same.' He shrugged as if he didn't get the connection at all. Elliott narrowed his eyes, checking Ben out. Was he having him on? Ben's expression remained vacant.

'Look,' Elliott said at last, 'just tell me if you're thinking of wandering off somewhere, eh?'

'Like where?'

Elliott couldn't help laughing, then said with enough edge to make sure Ben knew he meant it, 'Like somewhere you can't find your way out of. Somewhere you might get your head bashed in.'

'What are you on about?' Ben bristled. 'I can look after myself. You sound like Dad. What are you going to do? Follow me everywhere?'

'Maybe.'

'Into the toilet?'

'Yeah. If I have to. That's always when the ghosts get you, of course – when your pants are down.' Elliott waited for Ben to grin first, then said, 'Listen, I'm just saying this is weird stuff, so let's not go anywhere alone, OK?'

'There's no way some ghost of Eve made the noises last night,' Ben said dismissively. 'What do you think she's doing? Wandering about dragging her ugly dolly around?'

'I don't know,' Elliott answered honestly. 'It fits what we're reading. Have you got a better explanation?'

'Anything could have made that noise,' Ben argued. 'Plenty of other stuff.'

'Like what?'

'Like a million things.'

'So many you can't think of one, eh?' Elliott said. 'What about the old woman we saw? It's got to be Janey, hasn't it? There's her age, all the flowers on her dress, and she's living near us. It's got to be the same person.' And, as he said that, Elliott thought back to the way the woman had peered at him in the garden. There'd been nothing neighbourly about that stare of hers. He didn't want to admit any fear of her in front of Ben, but she'd unsettled him. The fact that Theo in the diary liked Janey didn't make Elliott feel any better about her.

'There are still some pages left,' he said to Ben. 'Do you want to read them now or later?'

'Now.'

20th October. I came across Mum outside today. She had her easel open, and was painting. The whole canvas was covered in a single light blue colour. Mum corrected me when I asked her about it. *Several shades* of blue, apparently.

'It's a portrait,' she said. 'Haven't you seen this colour before?'

I looked at the picture for a long time before I worked out what it was.

Of course. Janey's eyes.

'She's fascinating, isn't she?' Mum whispered, and something about the way she said it made me realise she'd been watching Janey a lot. 'It's the way she moves,' Mum said, lowering her brush. 'She's naturally graceful, but it's as if she's responding to something else as well. She's always in motion, have you noticed that? Always anticipating something. Her body's full of odd changes in direction, tilts and turns, which should look clumsy, but don't. She's poetry somehow.' Mum shook her head, laughing. 'And how on earth am I going to capture all of that on canvas?'

Mum got more serious later on, though, when Dad showed us both something. He'd come across a new sketch done by Eve. It was under her pillow. The words scrawled near the edge of the picture are bad enough.

To be killed by those you love

Scary or what? Eve says she read the line in a book somewhere, but she can't name the book. It's not one of her fluffy-bunny picture books, I can tell you that.

But the sketch itself is almost worse. I couldn't work out what it was of at first. Nor could Dad. Mum took less time than us, and when she figured it out she was really upset and tried to dismiss it. Here's why: the picture shows a man and woman lying dead underwater. And though Eve denies it, the drowned man and woman look suspiciously like Mum and

41

Dad. 'It's only a drawing,' Eve said when asked about it. 'But why did you do it?' Mum demanded. 'Why?' No answer.

Later, when I went up to see Eve in her room, I found her gazing at one of the portraits of the owner again. I hadn't realised before just how many portraits of him there are in the house. Whenever you look up there he is, smiling away with his big ugly teeth. Even when you're between rooms, he'll be grinning away at you from some hall or ceiling. It's impossible to get away from his gaze. I've watched Eve following the portraits from floor to floor, room to room. She always ends up outside the East Wing, looking inside.

But here's the weirdest thing – Mum's fascinated by the portraits as well. Being an artist herself, she's worked out all sorts of things about them, too. The biggest surprise to me is that – get this – the owner did all the portraits *himself*. The painting style is consistent with a single artist, apparently. And it couldn't have been someone else who painted them, she says, because if anyone had been commissioned to do so many boringly similar paintings there'd be signs of careless or rushed work.

'There's no evidence of that in any of the portraits,' Mum said. 'Every brush stroke is lingered over. The owner obviously couldn't wait to show us everything he'd killed and how good he felt about it.'

6

THE GRAVEYARD

Elliott stopped reading and gazed around him. So did Ben.

They were not alone. The owner stared back at them from a portrait on the nearest wall. He was also staring at them from a portrait on the farthest wall and from a miniature canvas over the dressing table. In this smaller portrait the owner had just killed a big freshwater pike fish. Its body was suspended from a steel hook jammed into its gills.

Elliott reached up to the portrait.

'What are you doing?' Ben said, stopping his arm.

'I'm taking it down.'

'Why?'

'Because I'm sick of seeing it. All right with you?'

Ben licked his lips uneasily and Elliott yanked on the wooden frame. The effort to prise it off brought his face close to another portrait.

The dead animal depicted in this one was a grey wolf. The picture was done in heavy spatula strokes, and this time the owner looked especially happy, especially pleased with his kill. His left hand was under the wolf's pelt, a single arm holding up its full deadweight. *He was strong*, Elliott realised, and for a moment he forgot what he'd been doing with the picture of the pike. He was in the process of placing it back on its mount again when he caught himself. Then, glancing at Ben, he stashed the portrait under an assortment of magazines.

Ben writhed uncomfortably, but said nothing.

Elliott went back to the diary.

25th October. Eve tore down the makeshift barrier leading into the East Wing today. Dad put it straight back up again and really told her off this time, but I'm not sure Eve was even listening.

Later, Mum found a whole new set of drawings. Eve's been busy. The drawings were all stuffed under her bed and *every single one* is a copy of the owner's portraits. When I mentioned it to Janey later she said matter-of-factly, 'They warned me this might happen. There hasn't been a child in the house for a long time.'

I stared at her. '*They* warned you? What are you talking about?'

She glanced at me warily, as if she wasn't sure I was ready to hear what she had to say. Then she

led me towards the graveyard in the north corner of the estate.

No one reading this diary is going to believe me, but this is exactly what happened next. Janey stood beside a broken headstone. She was looking at me with a weird smile on her face. Then she turned her head. From the way she did it I knew someone was close by, except . . . there was only empty space. Then, offering another sideways smile (but not to me), Janey nodded (again not to me), walked straight across and stroked my cheek.

I jumped back. I'd have pulled away completely, but Janey kept smiling at me, and her hand was delicate and warm as well, which was weird, because her fingers were gritty from touching the cold gravestone. Anyway, when I held her wrist to make her stop, she did. But as soon as I let her go again her fingers returned to my face, or wanted to. I found out later that someone else was guiding her hand. That was the only way she – it was a girl – was able to feel me. She had to do it via Janey.

'Stop running away. Let me finish,' Janey said, when I backed off.

'What the hell are you doing?' I shouted.

She grinned and looked behind her. 'Just because they're dead doesn't mean they're not interested,' Janey said. 'Theo, I'd like to introduce you to Nell

Smith. She's sixteen going on three-hundred and twenty. An admirer from afar. She counts four freckles on your forehead. She says there are too many to count on the rest of your face, but that if you stay still for a minute she'll try.'

I backed off fast. Seconds later, what looked like a stiff breeze came out of nowhere, and this time something seemed to invisibly clutch at Janey's legs. I hadn't really believed or understood the Nell stuff, hadn't taken in that it was a ghost Janey was so offhandedly talking about, but I didn't have time to think about it before Janey murmured, 'Here comes Leo. He's only small. A winter death. Watch out for the snow.'

I looked up, almost expecting white flakes, but Janey was joking about that part.

She sat down on the grass. As she tucked her knees under her, I saw a little depression form in her dress as something dived onto her lap. 'He's five,' she mouthed at me. 'He's still scared. All the time.'

Another ghost came after Leo. Someone taller this time, obviously older. Janey leaned back, allowing whoever it was to take her weight. She said something friendly under her breath. 'A farmer's boy,' she whispered to me. 'He died with his boots on. Hunted.'

47

He turned out to be a seventeen-year-old called Sam Cosgrove. Janey upped and went on a circular walk with him around the graveyard, and from the natural way she chatted to him I realised it was the sort of thing they did all the time. I was shocked, and really scared too, and Janey must have realised that, because she left me alone for a while. But the ghosts didn't leave her alone. They even followed her from the graveyard when we left, only stopping when we got near Glebe House.

Janey dropped virtually to the ground at one point to pick someone up from the grass. Soft words and smiles followed – plenty of smiles. I later found out that this ghost was a nine-year-old girl named Alice Everson.

'What ... what did you say to her?' I asked afterwards.

Janey shrugged. 'I said I loved her.' I must have looked confused. 'Haven't you ever told someone you love them?' she asked me. 'Something simple and truthful like that, if that's what they needed to hear?'

When I just stared at her like a dummy, Janey sighed. 'The ghosts only have each other, Theo. It's not quite enough. Hardly anyone living has my gift, and most of those who do are too afraid to use it. Or they stop using it because' – she gestured meaningfully towards her own house – 'it frightens people.'

7th November. Since then I've watched Janey a lot. I've seen that wherever she goes she's always reacting to the ghosts. There are four of them, all children – Sam, Nell, Leo and Alice – and they almost never leave her alone. Invited or not, they're always crowding her, demanding her time. They tug her fingers, lift her hair. I stayed near her for over an hour that first day, saying nothing, while she gave something to each of the children, touched and touching.

'It's . . .' Janey tried to explain what it was like having them around. 'It's like we're solid,' she said, poking my chest, 'while they are *not*.' She laughed. 'They're all movement, I mean. Like eels. All spirit. It's hard for them to stay still, even for a little while. They're meant to be on their way somewhere else. They're always fighting the journey there. They're all in motion from holding the journey back.'

She made a gesture, and a ripple like a dancing wave flowed through her. Then she touched her left hand to her temple and closed the fingertips of her other hand with a small quiet *snap*. I realised after hours of studying her that it was a kind of special language I was seeing, something she only shared with the ghosts. Later, I dazedly followed Janey to an area where wild daisies were growing under a hawthorn bush. Fitting one into a buttonhole of her dress, she said, 'This was Alice's favourite flower when she was alive.'

I thought I'd never really understand what was going on between Janey and the ghost children, but a few days later, November 5th, Guy Fawkes night, I decided to have a guess at what the ghosts were doing here. Dad had built a bonfire in the grounds, and I'd spent half the evening watching Janey's head swaying near the flames.

'The ghosts come for company, don't they?' I said hesitantly. 'They left life too soon, before they were ready. And because you have this gift, they come here, you know, because, well, there's no one else to talk to, and they're lonely.'

Janey laughed so hard that she honked. 'No, Theo,' she said. 'This isn't a romance or some sort of game. I'm not their dearest friend or anything. The ghosts are gathered here for one reason only.'

'What reason?'

'Right now, they're hassling me about you and Eve. It's been a long time since any kids came inside Glebe House.'

Janey saw my bewilderment.

'No, come on, tell me,' I demanded. 'What's this got to do with me and Eve?'

Janey folded her arms. 'Describe the ways children die, Theo.'

'What?' I was thrown by the question. 'I don't know. Mostly accidents, I suppose. Disease . . . Hunger. That sort of thing.'

'Or they're deliberately killed,' Janey said. 'Murdered. Of course, the four ghosts don't talk about the way they died very often. It's not something they like being reminded of. Only the original owner of Glebe House enjoys doing that, and he does so whenever he can. Whenever, that is, he gets close enough for the ghosts to hear his whisper.'

While I tried to take this in, Janey pointed at the perimeter walls.

'I'd like to be able to walk across the Glebe estate without gathering ghosts around me all day long,' she said grimly. 'But that won't happen until the hunter in the East Wing is stopped. The ghost children aren't pining to be alive, Theo. They don't wish to be with us at all. They should be elsewhere. The dead are meant to be dead. They've stayed behind on this spot because of what's inside Glebe House. To stop the owner who killed them from

killing anyone else. Right now – to stop him from killing you and Eve.'

'That's it,' Elliott said, laying the last sheet down.

'What? The diary ends there?' Ben groaned. 'You're kidding! There're no more pages?'

'I know. I can't believe it, either,' Elliott said, 'but it's all Dad could find.' He re-read the last entries. 'The original owner,' he murmured. 'Janey was telling Theo that he's still here in the house.'

'The same man who did the portraits?'

'Mm.'

Ben kneaded his bruise. 'Load of rubbish,' he grunted. 'This whole diary thing is made up. Has to be. Something Theo left behind as a laugh. Pretty clever, if you think about it.'

'Yeah, maybe,' Elliott said doubtfully, needing time to think.

'It's a story,' Ben insisted. 'It's got to be. Anything else is just stupid.' He stood up.

'Where are you going?' Elliott asked.

'To the bathroom. If I'm not back in five minutes you might want to check, though.'

'Check what?'

'That I'm still in there,' Ben said, grinning. '*Still alive*, I mean. Whooooooooooh!'

Ben laughed, but Elliott didn't join in, and after his

brother walked off Elliott sat on the edge of his mattress, still reeling from the diary revelations. Had Theo really made the whole thing up? Was it just the fact that he'd seen the older version of Janey Roberts, Theo's neighbour in the 1960s, that made the diary feel so real? Elliott wanted to believe that, but only because the alternative wasn't something he wanted to believe at all. Because if Theo was telling the truth, fifty years ago his little sister Eve had repeatedly gone into the East Wing. She'd become so obsessed with the owner's portraits that she'd gone as far as to smash her way inside. And now the same thing was happening to Ben. How likely a coincidence was that?

And something else was bothering Elliott. He didn't like to admit it, but he'd been drawn to the owner's portraits himself. He kept finding his gaze flicking up to them. In fact, knowing that the pike portrait was buried under all those magazines in his bedroom had been bothering him all the time he'd been reading the diary. He had a strong desire to return the painting to its proper place on the wall. The urge kept itching at him.

He was busy gathering together all the diary pages to show Dad when a sharp cry came from across the hall. Seconds later Ben came crashing into his room, running full-tilt. He arrived breathless and pale, but also fizzing with excitement.

'You're never going to believe this,' he gasped.

'Believe what?'

'No point telling you. It's amazing. Come and look.'

7
DO YOU WANT TO PLAY?

Ben was so eager to haul him into his room that when he got there Elliott expected to see, well, nothing less than a ghost. Instead, Ben's room seemed no different from normal. Elliott tried to keep himself calm while his eyes swept the room.

'It's Old Albert,' Ben said, as if only a blind man could miss it. He pointed at a big teddy bear sitting squarely in the middle of the bed.

'I didn't know you still had that ancient thing,' Elliott said.

'I haven't been playing with him, you idiot,' Ben said scathingly. 'He was in the box downstairs with all our old toys. I haven't touched him for years.'

'So what's he doing on your bed?'

'How do I know? When I came back he was *just there*.'

Elliott warily circled Old Albert, studying him from all angles. The teddy's fat hairy arms were sticking straight out. He looked desperately keen to be played with.

'Maybe Dad did it as a surprise? A joke,' Elliott said.

'Don't be dumb. Anyway, something's been playing with him.'

'Playing?'

'Look.' Without getting too close to Old Albert, Ben pointed at his head. 'There. See where he's been *brushed*? See the fur? It's all smooth. And the bow round his neck's been made ... I don't know ... prettier. Dad wouldn't do that. *We* didn't do it. It must be the ghost.'

Elliott felt his skin prickle. If it hadn't been for Theo's entries, and the scrishing sounds, he would never have taken the suggestion seriously. But an actual ghost in the house? Despite the diary, he wasn't quite ready to accept that.

'OK. Let's suppose you're right,' he said, mainly to give himself time to organise his thoughts. 'Let's suppose it is a ghost. What kind of ghost are we talking about here?'

'A child,' Ben said. 'Like in the diary.'

'OK,' Elliott agreed. 'A child, because who else would want to brush an old teddy?' The thought of that was briefly so ludicrous that he laughed.

'Not just a child,' Ben said, deadly serious. 'A girl. Teddies, so a *little* girl,' he added. 'In the diary Eve liked her dolls, remember? We haven't got any dolls. Old

Albert was probably the nearest thing she could find in the box.'

A real ghost girl? Elliott thought. It was hard to believe, but the evidence appeared to be on the bed. And if their ghost was playing with cuddly toys, it presumably must be young. Could it really be Eve? The diary gave no indication that Eve had died, but they only had a single fragment to go on. Maybe she'd died soon after the last entry. Had there been an accident? Dad said there'd been a tragedy here the owners didn't want to talk about . . .

'A little girl who wants to play,' Ben murmured. He gave Elliott an astonished look, as if he couldn't quite believe what he was saying. 'Are you scared?'

'Yes,' Elliott said. 'And stop pretending you're not.'

'I'm not *that* scared,' Ben growled back. 'How scary can a little girl be? But what's she doing here? And where's she been hiding all this time? We've been here three days now. Where's she been?'

'The East Wing, I suppose,' Elliott said. 'You went in there last night. You opened it, didn't you? Maybe you stirred something up. Our ghost might have been stuck in there all this time. But now it's out, and it wants to play.'

'I didn't make that hole into the East Wing!' Ben yelled.

'Are you sure?'

'Of course I am. I'm not lying! I didn't do it!'

Elliott wanted to believe him, but after reading Theo's diary he wasn't entirely convinced Ben was telling the truth. Eve had torn the barrier down without admitting to it as well. On the other hand, if Ben *was* telling the truth, then something had smashed its way out of the East Wing, and suddenly the idea of a ghost in the house, little girl or otherwise, didn't seem so harmless.

'Maybe we can . . . I don't know . . . find out what she's doing here,' Ben said breathlessly. 'You know, invite her to play. Find out about her. How she died.' He nodded to himself, squeezing his hands together. 'Yeah, why not?'

'What are you talking about?' Elliott said, trying to think. 'We're not playing with any ghosts. Anyway, if you were a ghost girl, stuck here, would you rather play with toys or play with *us*?'

'What do you mean?' Ben asked, taken aback.

'I mean, we're real. She'll probably be a whole lot more interested in you and me than in Old Albert.'

That quietened Ben down. In any case, Elliott could tell that Ben had no desire to play with ghosts, little girls or otherwise. He was only getting ready to do so in case one slipped into the room, giving him no choice.

A child wanting to play, Elliott thought, a small shiver running through him. The innocent way Ben said it, nothing could have sounded more natural. But if a *dead* little girl wanted to play, what did it mean? The same as with a living child? Or would a ghost child want to play in other ways? In dead ways? With dead things?

Elliott traced the lines of the decorative bow around Old Albert's neck. Only smaller fingers than Ben's could have tied it so neatly.

'Come on, we're getting out of here,' he said. 'Let's find Dad.'

He was about to lead the way when Ben grabbed his shirt. 'Wait,' he said. 'What's that?'

Elliott saw it now: a sheet of paper fluttering through the part-open door.

When it landed near them both boys, breathing hard, stood looking at each other for a moment. Then Ben tiptoed across to pick the sheet up.

In thick, red-pencilled letters, a child's non-joined-up style, someone had left them a message:

To my friends

Ben unfolded the note and brought it across to Elliott. The message inside was simple.

Do you want to play?

Ben threw the note down, backing away. 'It *is* a child!' he whispered. 'It might already be in the room with us.

Somewhere we can't see . . .' He kicked the bed.

Elliott didn't know what to think, but the only sensible thing to do was to get them both out of the room.

'It's OK,' he told Ben, gritting his teeth. 'I don't know what's outside, but we're going to leave together. Whatever's out there, we'll walk straight past it. Are you ready?'

Ben swallowed and nodded, and Elliott had just taken hold of his arm when they heard a scrishing noise.

'Get behind me,' Elliott ordered.

As Ben retreated, Elliott watched the doorway. Excited scrambling had started up outside, scurrying feet taking less than a second to run the whole length of the corridor and back. Elliott checked the window behind him. Dad was out there, a faraway dot in the southern grounds. Heading towards the glass, Elliott was getting ready to open the window when the bedroom doorway creaked a little wider.

Ben gasped as a shadow edged across the room. 'Shut the door!' he yelled. 'Elliott, don't just stand there! Shut it!'

But before Elliott could move another object was thrown inside the bedroom. It entered half way up the door this time, bouncing lightly across the carpet, *bump, bump*, before coming to rest near Ben's feet.

Elliott nearly collapsed with relief when he saw that it was only a scrunched-up ball of paper.

He opened it. Inside was a sketch. It was in Eve's style, as described in the diary, but different as well. Blockier. Darker. Done in pencil but so heavily that it looked more like charcoal.

It showed a boy asleep in bed, the stars visible through his bedroom window.

'It *is* Eve!' Ben hissed. He stared at the sketch, then gave Elliott an amazed look. 'It's a picture of ... that's me, isn't it? It's me sleeping in the new bed. *She's been watching us.*'

Sweat trickled down Elliott's neck as he gazed at the sketch. Then he looked up at the door, preparing himself for Eve to enter. 'Is it really you, Eve?' he whispered. No answer. Only swift, eager panting from the corridor outside.

Eyes wide with fear, Ben picked up a cup from the bedside table and threw it at the door.

Readying himself, Elliott said loudly, 'Whoever you are, I'm coming out.'

'Elliott, no!' Ben yelled. 'Stay here! Don't go out!'

A new noise from the corridor stopped Elliott in mid-stride: *scribbling*. Seconds later another tight wad of paper was thrown into the room.

'Don't touch it!' Ben said.

But Elliott had already walked into the centre of the

room and picked up the sheet of paper. It was another note.

Can I come in?

Such a simple question. Such a disarmingly simple question. But what reply to give? Say *yes* and whatever was in the corridor might come straight inside. They weren't ready for that. But how would it react if they said *no*?

'Say no!' Ben demanded. 'Go on, Elliott! Hurry! Say no! Write it down!'

Elliott scanned the room for a pen or pencil, couldn't find one. He was still deciding what to say when the visitor, clearing its throat, said something of its own.

8

A IS FOR ALICE

'A is for Alice, who fell down the stairs . . .'
It was a voice at last, but not the kind Elliott would have
expected. It sounded like a girl, but not quite. It was
gruff at the edges. And there was something truly
terrifying about that when you could not see the face.

' . . . B is for Bobby, all dead in his chair. C
is for Craig, who couldn't stay warm . . .'

The words flowed eerily, a sing-songy voice that could
easily have been either a girl's or a boy's. Or even a
man's, Elliott realised. Yes. It could have been a man
strangulating his throat to make himself sound younger.

'D is for David, under the lawn. E is for Eddie,
dragged and bound. F is Felicity, who never was
found . . .'

Fear sliced through Elliott. He couldn't decide: was
this a man contorting his voice to sound like a girl, or a
girl imitating a man by pitching her voice lower? But
why would a girl do something as weird as that? The
longer Elliott listened the more he sensed that they

might not be dealing with a child at all. More likely something that only sounded like a child. Something that wanted them to *think* it was a little girl.

'A is for Alice, who fell down the stairs . . .'

Elliott recognised that name as the nine-year-old ghost-girl in Theo's diary, but the other names were new. Had the owner been responsible for more deaths than the four mentioned in the diary? The rhymes ran sequentially through the alphabet, and Elliott steadied himself to listen.

'. . . G is for Guy, crushed under a horse. H is for Henry, broken of course. J is for Jane, now ageless and white, and also for Jack, at the end of his fight . . .'

'Where's Dad?' Ben whispered. 'It's him singing, isn't it? It must be.'

'Shush,' Elliott murmured. 'You know it's not Dad.'

'. . . and also for John, once quiet and tall. And L is for Leo, who gave his all. M is for . . .'

Elliott didn't wait to find out who 'M' was. He ran towards the door and kicked it open.

A ghost stood outside.

It was Eve. Although her skin was utterly grey, it was definitely her. Definitely the girl from the diary sketch. But what had happened to her? She looked wild. Her matted hair was plastered in a tangled blonde mess over her cheeks, her teeth clenched in a vast fury. Stamping the ground, she shook a tiny enraged fist at them.

Her doll, Katerina, lay next to her on the hallway floor. Eve picked Katerina up by her feet and swung her solid plastic head at Elliott, *swoop swoop*, like a battering ram.

Elliott barely knew what he was saying, he was so frightened. 'It's ... it's OK ...' he stuttered.

Eve stared not at Elliott, but at Ben. There was a child's curiosity contained in that stare, but it was violent too, floating in its own raw well of meaning. Yet it was unquestionably a little girl they were looking at. It was certainly Eve and, though her red dress was filthy, it was still a little girl's dress, nothing worse. And when she dropped her angry pose and suddenly whispered a heartfelt *Help me, help me, please*, before abruptly twisting around and running off, Elliott found himself following her to see where she went.

Eve was fast. Her feet, spilling dust, hardly touched the floorboards. With that pitiable *help me* ringing in his ears, Elliott guessed where she was heading and ran towards the East Wing. He got there just in time to see Katerina being carted through the entrance.

'It's OK!' Elliott called out. 'Eve, we're not going to hurt you. Don't go. Please ...'

Before he thought about what he was doing, he'd leapt inside the East Wing. He only stopped running down its corridors when Eve did.

'It's OK,' he said, catching his breath. 'We'll ... we'll help you.'

Eve had come to a halt and was now crouched against the far end of a corridor. Her back was to Elliott. Pressing her cheek hard against the wall, she whispered, 'S is for Sandra, burning bright, T for Tobias, a swish of the scythe. And also for Tanya, who writhed and writhed . . .'

Listening, Elliott realised that while it had taken Eve only *one single second* to run the whole length of the corridor upstairs, she'd let him keep up on the way to the East Wing. She obviously wanted him to follow her inside.

Eve stayed entirely still. 'E is for Elliott, all alone, all alone . . .'

'It's OK ...' Elliott said hollowly, his voice fading away in fear. Suddenly the last thing he wanted was for Eve to turn around. 'I ... we won't hurt you.'

Eve let out a quiet, lonely moan. Then she turned to face him.

The fighter's stance was gone. Replacing it was a sly smile. The smile played on Eve's lips and, widening it, she gave Elliott a performer's curtsey, as if she was about to show him something spectacular.

'Don't,' Elliott said, fearing what she was going to do.

'It's OK,' she said, calmly reversing their roles – a child deciding to comfort him.

But she wasn't really comforting him, Elliott decided. She was just reassuring him to keep him there, to make sure he watched.

Eve opened out her hands, like a magician showing him she had nothing concealed. And then, bringing her arms down, finger-curves winding across her dress, as if unravelling it, her whole body dissolved into the wall, leaving only a trail of dark, dust-smeared light. Inside that residue of light she left her two eyes a moment. They blinked: once, twice. Then they, too, pressed forward, following the rest of her body into the wall.

Katerina clattered to the floor, left behind.

Elliott was too afraid to move for a moment. Then he shakily walked across the floor and prodded Katerina. Solid plastic. Heavy. Real. He picked her up. She smelled of stale carpet and ingrained dirt, and her plastic face was pitted and scratched from years of being dragged over countless surfaces.

Dropping her, Elliott twisted around. It was only when he looked back over his shoulder up the corridor that he realised he couldn't remember the turnings that had brought him this far into the East Wing.

9

THE EAST WING

A nondescript and almost perfectly straight corridor stretched ahead of Elliott. Though his heart was still thumping, nothing about the corridor looked menacing and he decided to treat it that way. He didn't panic. He knew he hadn't gone far inside the East Wing. How hard could it be to find the exit?

The corridor he was in lacked true windows, but sunshine filtered through narrow angular slits in the high ceiling. What Elliott did not know was that the original owner had built just enough illumination into the East Wing to keep its guests on the move.

His first few entangling steps led him to a branching four-way intersection. From the crossing paths he saw that he could go straight ahead, left or right. Or back, of course. He could always go back. But which way was correct? The corridors radiating from the intersection were all the same height and width. The walls were indistinguishably white-grey.

Keeping a guarded look out for Eve, Elliott breathed

in the dry musty air. *So easy to get lost here*, he realised.

A crack of sunlight lit up an oil painting on the nearest wall. It was one of the owner's self-portraits, and Elliott leaned forward to take a closer look.

The painting showed a hunting scene. No surprise there, given the portraits he'd seen elsewhere in the house. But this portrait wasn't like the scenes in the main property. Those all showed dead birds, hogs, deer or other animals. What Elliott was looking at now was a picture of the owner hunting a girl. Not chasing her. Hunting her.

The girl looked to be around sixteen years old, and Elliott could tell from her frightened expression that this was no game. In the portrait, the owner's face – beard freshly combed and oiled – shone with anticipation.

With his pulse racing, Elliott stood in front of the portrait for over a minute. Then he spotted another difference between this portrait and those elsewhere. Outside the East Wing the owner was always standing stiff and at attention with his weapons and kills beside him. Here the paintwork was freer. The owner's red hair flowed in the picture, the enjoyment obvious in his upturned eyes. This was clearly a hunt he'd savoured. His scissored legs were striding up a steep muddy slope fringed by trees, and the girl did not look as if she would escape.

Blinking uneasily, Elliott examined another painting in the same corridor.

Again there was the slope. Again the trees. Again a person being chased. This time, however, it was a woman. In another painting the owner was running after a pair of men. Two strong men they were, and they'd been roped together, as if to make it harder for them to fight or to get away. In another canvas, bizarrely, the owner was hunting himself. That was the only painting where the hunter and the hunted both looked amused.

With a sinking feeling in his gut as he gazed at the landscape in all the paintings, Elliott realised, *It's a hunting ground.*

Dotting the length of the East Wing's corridors, between the paintings, were doors. There were always four doors to a corridor, and all the doors were composed of plain wood with the same brass handles. Elliott picked a door at random in the hope of finding an exit. The brass handle felt smooth and surprisingly warm as he twisted it. The door opened invitingly.

Inside, he discovered a fully-furnished bedroom. The next room along the corridor was also a bedroom, decorated the same way. The third and fourth rooms were almost identical to the first.

Elliott walked dazedly between them, finding barely any variations.

At the back end of each room there was always another door, which led into a further corridor. And that corridor in turn always led to more doors that were all alike and ever willing to open to Elliott's hand.

Nothing was closed off to him. Everything opened. Everything allowed you in.

With a shiver of fear pooling in his stomach, Elliott instinctively yelled 'Dad!' as loudly as he could. His voice did not travel far. The East Wing's absorbent carpets and thickly-papered walls hushed everything. No one on the outside could hear you in this place.

In the next corridor he found a note on the floor. It was in Eve's handwriting.

> Five minutes to midnight,
> Mark the time.
> Let the hunt begin
> With a little rhyme.

Elliott quickly twisted around, thinking she might be behind him. The corridor was empty, but suddenly Elliott wondered if he could outrun Eve if he had to. No, he decided. He'd seen how fast she was. Eve knew the layout of the corridors as well, the shortcuts. *She's not just a little girl*, he realised. *No one could live inside here for fifty years and stay a little girl.*

Had she deliberately led him in here so he would get lost? Once that thought lodged in his mind, Elliott couldn't shake it.

Arriving at another four-way intersection, he glanced up to see the most frightening portrait so far. It showed a boy of about five or six years old. He was wearing a bright blue cape, and his little legs were running as hard as they could up the slope of the hunting ground. Below him, the owner was not yet following. Instead, he was busy attaching heavy objects to each of his thighs. Elliott squinted, trying to work out what the objects were. Finally he realised that they were weights.

The owner was manacling big chunks of stone and metal to his legs.

Why was he doing that? Dread cut through Elliott as an answer came to him: *To make it harder.* This was a small child. The owner was adding the weights to make the chase more even.

The possibility that he might be anywhere near the spirit of a person who would do something as horrifying at that made Elliott stop in his tracks.

Rather than blunder on, he formulated a new plan. The portraits. Why not use them to navigate? Each was different. If he memorised those at the start of corridors he could avoid entering the same corridor twice. By elimination he was bound in the end to find the one that led out of the East Wing.

And now the first real game began, because it felt so possible. Elliott set about it diligently, memorising portrait subjects at the intersections. A hunted woman. Another woman with a mask over her face. A man running, the owner attacking him with a scythe. Another similarly dressed man, but the scythe this time in the owner's other hand.

It seemed easy at first. Surely he could do this. But there were so many intersections and pictures, and the contrasts between them were often so subtle, that only someone able to memorise perfectly could succeed. The owner had tested this during his lifetime. He'd let dozens of people loose like spiders inside the East Wing and seen who crawled out. If they managed it he found out how, and made corrections until almost no one could.

The first sign that Elliott was beginning to panic came when he started calling out Eve's name. He'd never have done so at the beginning. He was too afraid of her then. But at some point he'd crossed a threshold where he was more frightened of being stuck alone inside the East Wing than of anything a ghost girl, no matter how sinister, could do to him.

'Hello? Eve? I've read Theo's diary ... My name's Elliott ...'

He made another turn, right this time. Then, because he had to try something different, he pushed

73

open more doors. None were locked. All led to the same repetition of bedrooms. Surely Ben and Dad had to be looking for him by now, Elliott thought. Then he remembered that Ben hadn't seen him enter the East Wing.

He stopped for a moment, aware that he was shaking. *You're OK*, he told himself, knowing it wasn't true.

'Are you there, Eve? I'm a friend. I won't hurt you . . .'

Elliott travelled on, and with every step the East Wing's rich burgundy carpet welcomed his feet with cushioning silence.

Several corridors later, another turn led him somewhere new.

Elliott stopped, holding his breath.

In front of him the floor descended. At the end of that descent was a small staircase. At the end of that staircase was a dark passageway.

At first sight the dark passageway looked no different from the other gloomy corridors Elliott had already walked down. But somehow it was. He waited until the difference was clearer. There were two differences. One, the passageway had no slit-windows, making it much darker than elsewhere. Two – he wasn't sure. There *was* another difference, but he couldn't quite name it.

Staring into the passageway's depths, Elliott realised that he was trembling.

'Eve?'

The dark passageway was an impenetrable, unyielding black. It was depths upon depths of darkness. Was this where Eve had been leading him all along? Surely his own meandering footsteps had brought him here? But Elliott couldn't be sure of that. All he knew was that nothing, absolutely nothing, would convince him to enter that passageway.

Summoning all his reserves of strength, he turned around and, one dread-filled footstep at a time, walked away. Numerous choices of corridors and rooms later, with his skin now stippled by cold, prickling sweat, Elliott's eyes snapped wide.

He couldn't believe it. Ahead of him the corridor descended. At the end of that descent was a small set of steps . . . leading to a dark passageway.

The next moment Elliott was running headlong. He couldn't stop himself. He was lost and running flat out. And abruptly it was as if it was not him running at all, but another child, a child being chased, a child from the past, a child who could not stop screaming.

And then a band of dazzling light suddenly unfurled across the walls ahead of him.

Like a drowning man, Elliott focused on it. Was it by luck, by chance, that he found his way out? Elliott didn't care. All he knew was that the next turn led him towards the ragged hole in the East Wing entrance. He hauled himself through it, and with a yell of sheer relief staggered into beautiful bright sunshine.

10

THE HUNTING GROUND

For several minutes Elliott crouched outside the East
Wing's entrance, simply getting his breath back, shaking
uncontrollably.

He couldn't believe how frightened he was. He hadn't
been pursued while he was inside the East Wing, but at
a subconscious level he knew that he'd been hunted. The
jaunty smiles from the portraits kept flashing into his
mind.

When he finally got his shattered nerves back
together, he heard a thin voice calling out, and realised it
was his own. Moments later Dad and Ben were running
towards the entrance.

'We looked for you!' Ben cried, rushing up to him.
'We did! We searched everywhere ...'

Elliott nodded, too frazzled to manage anything
else.

Dad's first reaction was anger. 'Didn't I tell you not
to go in there?' But as soon as he saw the state Elliott
was in, his expression changed completely. He steadied

his still-shaking shoulders. 'What happened? You got lost in there, didn't you?'

Elliott fumblingly told him everything, and it must have come out more emotionally than he intended because at some point Dad briefly held him.

Elliott shut his eyes for a few seconds, then looked at Dad again. 'You don't believe we saw a ghost, do you?'

Dad kept his hands on his shoulders. 'I know you saw something,' he said cautiously. 'I believe that.'

'He hasn't read the diary yet,' Ben muttered. 'We were too busy looking for you.'

'Read it, Dad,' Elliott told him and, marching him upstairs, he stuffed the pages into his hands. '*Read the whole thing.*'

Dad did so. When he'd finished the last page his eyes, creased with concern, came to rest slowly on both boys.

'All right,' he said hesitantly. 'I don't know what's going on here, but this' – he raised the diary – 'plus whatever you just saw in your room, and the East Wing …' Dad wavered, gradually coming to a decision. 'OK, here's what's going to happen. Until I understand what's going on in this house, I'm getting the two of you out. I'll have to temporarily seal the place up again. That'll take a day or so. But then we're gone, at least until I'm satisfied it's safe.'

He drew both boys closer to him. 'This little girl …' Elliott could see how difficult it was for Dad to believe in dead little girls, saw him searching for a simpler, more logical explanation. ' ... This Eve,' he continued. 'Are you sure she matched the description of the girl in the diary?'

'Yes,' Elliott and Ben said together.

'It was the same girl? You're certain?'

'Definitely,' Ben insisted.

'In that case,' Dad said turning towards him, 'I need to understand exactly what happened to you in the East Wing last night. Did you just fall over in the dark when you went inside? Or is there something else I should know?'

Ben clammed up, his face pale. When it was obvious he wasn't prepared to say anything more, Dad exchanged a concerned private look with Elliott and drew him aside. 'I wonder if the old woman you saw outside the garden, Jane Roberts, knows anything about what's going on?' he said. 'She seems to be the same one as in the diary.'

Elliott had been thinking along the same lines. 'Yeah, we should ask her,' he agreed. 'If the diary's telling the truth, she's linked to the ghosts somehow. She can't live too far away. She was on foot when we saw her.'

Dad nodded. 'I'll make some calls.' Then he gave Elliott a measured gaze. 'I've no idea what's going on around here, but are you OK to stay with Ben for a while?'

'Sure.'

'A ghost,' Dad said, shaking his head.

'We *did* see her,' Elliott told him firmly. 'I thought she needed help. That's what she told us.'

'So you went in the East Wing after her?'

'I know it was stupid . . .' Elliott began, thinking Dad was criticising him.

Dad placed a hand on his shoulder. 'Yes, it was stupid, but it took guts as well. Going after her into the East Wing like that. I'm not sure I'd have done it.'

That surprised Elliott. He'd never known anything frighten Dad.

'Twice I've been inside that place,' Dad said. 'Both times I was out again in less than five minutes. Looking at those portraits, I wonder if there was anything the owner didn't hunt. Or *want* to.' And as he said that, a pinch of fear settled over Dad's face. Elliott didn't like seeing it. The timing made him feel strangely vulnerable.

Together they led Ben back to Elliott's room. Dad took the room next door. 'I'll make the calls from in here,' he said. 'Shout if you need me.'

Elliott removed his trainers and sat on one of the antique, upholstered chairs near the window of his room. He was still shaking from his ordeal inside the East Wing. He kept seeing the owner's knee on the rise, the willingness of the land to receive his booted foot.

Next door he could hear Dad's urgent voice on the phone. Ben, on the other hand, was quiet and subdued. Elliott tried talking to him about Eve, but Ben didn't want to talk about anything to do with her, and Elliott decided to leave him alone for now. Eventually, though, it was Ben who broke the silence. 'Oh, I forgot to tell you,' he said. 'I found something on the fourth floor.'

'What?'

'It's a special portrait of the owner. I came across it when I was looking for you.'

Making sure Dad knew where they would be, Elliott let Ben lead him upstairs. In an out-of-the-way bedroom, tucked in an alcove, concealed behind a screen, was a large painting of a teenage boy.

'How did you find this?' Elliott asked.

Ben shrugged, gazing vaguely at the floor. 'I'm not sure. I just followed the other pictures.' He looked puzzled. 'They sort of led me to it.'

The painting was of a boy. A boy around seventeen years old, wearing heavy outdoor clothing. His mud-crusted brown boots were tucked inside padded baggy trousers. Elliott recalled Janey's words from the diary. '*Sam Cosgrove. A farmer's boy. He died with his boots on. Hunted.*'

Was this him? Elliott sensed it was.

The hunting ground was familiar to Elliott by now from his time in the East Wing. There it was, the slope and woods, awaiting the pursuit. But this time the owner hadn't yet started up the slope. He'd delayed the chase to record the *emotion* of the scene. Specifically, Sam Cosgrove's emotion.

At first Elliott thought the owner was missing from the picture. Then he realised his mistake. The owner was as present as ever. Only this time he was *reflected in Sam's wide dark eyes*. As Elliott leaned forward, the owner seemed to lean forward with him. His body was set in a crouch. Stripped down to shirt sleeves, he was coming at Sam with his bare hands, his enjoyment of the scene caught with relish.

Elliott gasped, pulling back. It was, he realised, a statement of intent. The owner was brashly declaring that he did not always hide behind traditional weapons like guns and blades. Sometimes, he was saying, when I hunt in private, *I alone* am the weapon.

The picture was damaged. At some point in the past a knife had been slashed through it. Deliberately? It looked like it, because the cut went right through the middle of Sam's lower face. It made his exact expression unreadable. Oddly, however, the damage to the canvas itself appalled Elliott as much as what had happened to Sam Cosgrove. He wanted to repair the painting. Fix it. Briefly that was more important to him than anything else.

Shaking that ridiculous thought from his head, Elliott looked across at his brother.

Ben seemed unaffected by the portrait. 'I've found the slope and the woods as well,' he said matter-of-factly. 'You can see them from upstairs.'

A dazed Elliott allowed Ben to guide him to the fifth floor.

And there it was, in plain sight – the hunting ground. It wasn't concealed or hidden away. It was a broad hillside surrounded by woods within easy walking distance of Glebe House. The topography of the land simply made it hard to recognise from the lower floors.

Nothing had significantly changed in all the years since the hunting ground's depiction in the paintings. The woods ranged around the slope were still extensive. If anything, the hunting ground seemed to have grown since the owner's time, the trees fuller, more numerous. The only major difference was that the cleared slope was now strewn with meadow-grass.

Seeing the hunting ground confirmed as real and *still there* made all the hairs rise on Elliott's neck. It was also obvious now why the owner had included the trees as well as the slope as part of his killing territory. The slope alone simply wasn't large enough for a proper pursuit. It was only a short scurry to get up the bank, at least for a strong adult. The owner might have used that for a quick chase and hack-down, but for a true contest he needed the woods as well. The thick trees fringing the slope offered a chance for his prey to hide, or even escape. Much more interesting.

Turning away in disgust, Elliott looked at Ben ... and found him standing utterly, utterly still. His arms were relaxed and by his side. Elliott realised that he had been standing like that, staring raptly at the hunting ground, ever since they entered the room. He also noticed for the first time a snag of tell-tale dust in Ben's hair.

'When did you go back into the East Wing?' he demanded, shocked.

'I ... I was searching for you, remember?' Ben said guardedly.

'You never told me you went into the East Wing.'

'Well I did, OK? I thought you'd gone in after Eve, but I wasn't sure. I wanted to go inside. To help you, I mean.' A confused expression crossed Ben's face. 'In the end all I found in there was ... well, I'll show you.'

He led Elliott back downstairs to his own bedroom. Swiping Old Albert off the mattress, Ben reached up to the mantelpiece. Several loose sheets of paper were there. Elliott recognised the writing style at once.

'Is that the bit of the diary we gave Dad to read?'

'No.' Ben gazed at him innocently. 'It's the next part.'

Elliott snatched the pages off him. 'Where did you find it?'

'It was just lying on the floor in the East Wing.'

'It wasn't there when I was inside,' Elliott said suspiciously. 'I'd have seen it.'

Ben looked genuinely confused. 'It's dark in there. You must have missed it. The diary was just lying right in front of me when I went in. The pages were all mixed up, but I've sorted them out.'

Elliott stared at Ben. 'Hold on. Are you saying that you didn't go to find Dad after we saw Eve? That first you went into the East Wing again, found these, took the time to get the pages in the right order, brought them up here, and only *then* went to look for Dad?'

Ben nodded. Elliott could tell that Ben saw nothing wrong with the sequence in which he'd done things. What was going on with him? Shaking his head, Elliott fingered the pages. 'Have you read them?' he asked. 'Did you do *that* before looking for me as well?'

'No.' Ben's face was expressionless.

'So let's do it,' Elliott said in bewildered exasperation. 'Let's read them.'

'All right.'

But Ben seemed to be in no hurry to get started. He was distracted, his gaze constantly being drawn to the nearest portrait. Elliott recognised it. The pike fish. It had not been in Ben's room earlier. It was meant to be hidden under magazines in Elliott's own bedroom. Ben had obviously taken it from there and added it to his personal collection of portraits. That collection seemed to be growing. No less than six paintings of the owner gazed down from the walls now.

'Why did you put the picture of the pike up?' Elliott asked him nervously.

Ben just shrugged.

Feeling his pulse quicken, Elliott turned to the diary. The first entry started the day after the last. Nothing was missing. But the tone was different. Previously the diary had contained jokes, unusual facts, as well as occasional references to events taking place in the village. Now only two subjects retained the attention of the increasingly frightened diarist, Theo Stark.

II

JANEY

9th November. No matter what Mum and Dad say to her, Eve keeps going inside the East Wing. 'It's no accident,' Janey told me this morning. 'It's not the mystery of the dark Eve finds so alluring. She's not being naughty, Theo. It's *him*. It's Cullayn, murmuring from inside. Always the hunter.'

'Cullayn?'

'The original owner,' Janey said grimly. 'The man who built the East Wing and did all those paintings your mum's starting to admire so much. Vincent Cullayn. The murderer of Alice, Sam, Leo and Nell. And a lot more adults.'

While I stood there blinking in shock, Janey took my hand and walked us across the estate. On the way she told me about Alice Everson. Alice died in 1689. Officially she fell down some stairs while delivering a message to a labourer in one of Cullayn's outbuildings. But what really happened, the ghost version of Alice told Janey, was that Cullayn carried her off to his hunting ground. He let her loose on it, counted slowly to *one thousand* and then went after her.

Nell Smith was found lifeless in the kitchen of the main house. Everyone thought she'd been working alone there for hours. In fact, Cullayn had snatched her out, carried her to the hunting ground and brought her back to the kitchen while she was still freshly dead.

'But ... but why did he kill them?' I asked, unable to believe what Janey was telling me.

'He liked killing,' Janey said evenly. 'Who can say why anyone enjoys something like that? Sam thinks it started with the animals – Cullayn had always brutally hunted those. Then one day a troublesome farm hand disappeared, and doing away with him seems to have given Cullayn a taste for murder. The deaths and disappearances gradually escalated after that. The four kids Cullayn took made a nice change for him from the adults. Easy prey, of course, but it also gave Cullayn the opportunity to be creative. He invited Leo Jenkins into his study. While he was there Cullayn offered him a little gift: a bright blue cape. Leo was a bit surprised when Cullayn began hanging heavy bits of metal on his own legs and shoulders, though. Cullayn loaded himself down with so many weights for Leo that he could barely stagger up the slope of his own hunting ground.'

I stared in horror at Janey. 'But I don't understand,' I said. 'Why ... why wasn't he stopped?'

'Because he was careful,' Janey explained. 'Cullayn owned several estates in this part of the country, and he made sure there was never more than a victim or two per season. Nothing too obvious. A drowning. Someone burning in a fire. A man falling unseen from his horse, and then crushed to death.' Janey shrugged. 'Some people just went missing. A wife disappears, but her husband is known to be violent. A young man vanishes, but so what? He was the ambitious type, and not liked anyway. Cullayn kept his eyes and ears open for opportunities like that.

'But Sam became suspicious, and followed Cullayn one time,' Janey went on. 'Saw him hunting on the slope. There was still no proof, though. The woman involved just *disappeared*. It was Sam's word against Cullayn's. Sam himself disappeared shortly after. No one knows what happened to him, but I do.' Janey shivered. 'Cullayn brought him to the hunting ground. Welcomed him in his own special way.

'That's how Cullayn got caught, in fact,' Janey

89

said. 'He was so furious with Sam that he was careless, left clues. When people finally came to get Cullayn for Sam's murder – they found no evidence he'd killed anyone else – Cullayn led them on a merry hunt all over the Glebe estate. They never found him.' Janey clicked her fingers. '*Pff*. He vanished. Squirmed his way out of his hanging. But the children know where he went. Cullayn died inside the East Wing. An accident, actually.' Janey smiled. 'You see, he had a secret room inside one of the walls. While everyone was searching for him, Cullayn hid himself in there for months. He only slipped out at night to take food and water from stashes he'd set aside on the estate in case he got caught. From outside, the secret room was opened by a pressure point on the wall. But inside the room there was just a simple lever. Cullayn used it once too often. The lever snapped off, and he couldn't fix it. He died of thirst, you'll be pleased to hear.'

I followed Janey in a daze across the southern grounds. She stopped to peer sharply up at the main house. Letting go of my hand, she turned to face me.

'Cullayn's an incredibly dangerous spirit,' she murmured. 'Normally only the ghosts of children can remain with us in our world. Even for them it's a hard thing to do, but for adults the pull of the other side is too strong to resist. Their spirits leave quickly. Cullayn, though, built the Glebe estate out of his own brutal desires, and somehow he's managed to keep himself here. And he's still hunting.'

'How?'

'By encouraging children inside. Children like Eve. If he can capture her spirit at the point of death he can feed off her. Use her energy to boost his own. He's stuck here for now, close to where he died. But if he can get energy from another ghost he might even be able to escape and carry on hunting beyond the Glebe estate.' Janey pursed her lips. 'The ghost children are constantly having to hide from Cullayn. They evade him by *staying still*. But doing that's hard for them, Theo. They're spirit-things. If the air moves they want to move with it. Cullayn looks for that motion when he drifts across the grounds.'

'But why don't they just leave?' I asked.

'I keep encouraging them to,' Janey said. 'To just go, pass on to the other side, get away from Cullayn. But they won't. Not while he's still here.' Janey shivered as a breeze came up. 'The truth is that the ghost children have been waiting all this time for someone like *me* to come along,' she said quietly. 'Someone able to hear and see them. That way they can at least warn us. So far Cullayn hasn't killed anyone since he died, but the ghost children think it's only a matter of time before he does. And he seems to have taken a particular interest in Eve. He's been more active than ever recently. The ghost children aren't sure why. But they're trying to protect you by warning me. Cullayn's already influencing Eve. You've seen that. He can't touch the living. Not physically. But he still has influence. He's dead, but the hunt goes on. It's all in the portraits. They're calling Eve closer. Even if you can't hear them, they're whispering. And they're inviting you, too, Theo.'

'Me?'

'Don't pretend you haven't caught yourself looking at them,' Janey said. 'Eve's just easier to influence. That's why Cullayn's concentrating on her. But listen ...' Janey took a sharp breath. 'Because of my talent, skill, whatever you want to call it, I've discovered something. I've realised I can do more than just warn people. I can be a weapon against Cullayn as well.'

'A weapon?'

Janey nodded eagerly. 'There are tricks, ways to pierce Cullayn's little realm. Ways to attack him. I'm learning all the time. Things the ghost children can't do, or won't, but maybe *I can*.'

Janey gave me an uncertain smile. 'I'm going after him, Theo. I'm not ready yet, but I won't let Cullayn hide forever. He's like a snake, waiting inside the East Wing, biding his time. Eve offers him the promise of far more fresh energy than the ghost children can give him after all these years dead. To get it, Cullayn's doing everything he can to make sure she dies within his reach. If he can take Eve's spirit for himself he'll become much more powerful. He's still incredibly ambitious. He intends to leave this place and take his hunt to the wider world. That's what Cullayn wants. To hunt forever, wherever he feels like it. But to get away from the Glebe estate he needs Eve dead. And he probably needs you, too.'

'Me?'

'Yes, you,' Janey growled. 'Stop thinking it's only Eve's who's in danger. Adults are no good to Cullayn. He'll kill your parents if he gets half the chance – he'll do that just for fun – but their spirits slip too fast across the divide for him to capture their energy. There's a moment of hesitation before the other side takes a child, though. It's you and Eve he needs. Cullayn will have an opportunity then, at the point of death. He just has to be there when it happens. And to be sure of that he needs to *make it happen*.' She gripped my arm. 'No, it's OK, don't worry, I won't let him hurt either of you,' she said. 'So far Cullayn's stayed away from me. I think it's because he's scared of what I can do to him. He feels safe tucked up in the East Wing, but why should he?' She lifted her chin. 'I'm going after him.'

15th November. That was a week ago. I wrote everything down and told Mum and Dad. I got Janey to talk to them as well. Did they take us seriously? Yes. Sort of. They asked a few locals about the history of the house and, apparently, though there aren't any details, there *were* deaths long ago, and Vincent Cullayn was held responsible for at least one of them.

'So you believe Janey, then?' I asked Mum.

'I believe at least one person was murdered here, yes,' Mum said, choosing her words carefully. 'That Janey believes Cullayn's evil spirit is still here as well ... yes, I can see Janey believes that, too. But I'm sorry, Theo. I know she's convinced you, but as for Eve, all that strangeness over the East Wing's stopped, hasn't it? I've never seen her having more fun. She loves it here. I don't think I've ever seen her happier.'

And the trouble is that Mum's right. Eve's totally changed. She's drawing nice happy pictures again. No more wandering off to the East Wing, either. She's even taken to joining Mum in the lake every morning for a swim. Eve always hated water before but lately, even though it's cold, she keeps wanting to paddle in the shallows. All this week she and Mum have been out there, splashing and laughing away.

Feeling a weight on his shoulder, Elliott glanced down. Ben was asleep against him. Perhaps the warmth of the room had made him drowsy. Or perhaps there were other reasons he would rather sleep than read on.

Elliott felt a force drawing his face to look up at the portraits on the walls. He resisted it, turning back to the last page of the diary.

24th November. Janey was forced to go away for a week to visit relatives with her parents. As soon as she got back I told her about Eve's new interest in swimming. She immediately rushed me up to an annex on the second floor of the main house. There's a portrait of Cullayn up there in a side room. I'd never seen it before. In the painting Cullayn's wearing long striped shorts, and proudly holding up a swimming trophy.

'His own competition,' Janey scoffed. 'He held it every year. He tended to win. Cullayn swam every day on the lake. Sam Cosgrove says he often went for a swim before a hunt as well. A cleansing ritual.'

I found myself peering closely at the picture. It was fascinating the life-like way the water was dripping from Cullayn's red beard, the drops glistening, clinging to his chin, almost as if . . .

'Don't!' Janey stepped in front of me. 'See? See!' She snapped her fingers in my face. 'I told you it's not just Eve being influenced. He's doing it to you as well. Don't you get it, Theo? He'd love to have you in his power, doing his killing for him.' She waved her hand in front of my face. 'He wants to cast a spell over you.'

She knocked the swimming portrait off the wall. When the fragile old wooden frame hit the ground it broke. I gasped, scandalised, but before I could stop her Janey went further, jabbing a sharp fingernail into the canvas and deliberately tearing at it, ripping away Cullayn's face.

'The paintings are worth a fortune!' I roared, fighting her for the picture. 'They're—'

'Shut up!'

'But they're not ours!' I shouted. 'They belong to the property. You can't—'

'Listen to you!' Janey danced away, keeping the picture out of my reach. 'Look how much you want to protect it! You can't even bear me touching it, can you?'

'Just give me the picture!'

I was furious. All I wanted to do in that moment was mend the portrait and hang it back on the wall. I couldn't stand the thought of anything else damaging it.

Janey refused to hand it over. 'I've told you all about him and you *still* want to protect it,' she said. 'Strange, eh? But it's not just you. It's everyone. Look at the East Wing. Filthy, ugly place it is, everyone's terrified of it, but it's been preserved. The ghost children tell me that not one portrait has been moved inside it since Cullayn died. Don't you think that's odd, Theo?'

I breathed in heavily, forcing back my anger. Even now I wanted to make sure no more harm came to the swimming portrait. Janey finally handed it back to me, and I managed to patch it up, jamming the frame joints together again.

Janey leaned back, watching me closely as I repositioned the picture on the wall. It was only then, glancing at her out of the corner of my eye, that I noticed something unexpected. I saw that Janey wasn't half as calm as she pretended to be. Both her hands had a white-knuckle grip on the wall. She was having to make a real effort to look away from the canvas. Her gaze was drawn towards it just like mine was and, though she spat on it when she saw me looking, and smiled defiantly, I knew then that even Janey wasn't immune to Cullayn's influence.

12

UNTIL MY WILL
MATCHES HIS

The diary extract ended with that line. Elliott flipped the page over, desperate for it to continue.

Ben, wide awake again, was reading over his shoulder. 'There are a few more,' he said.

'A few more what?'

'Pages of the diary.'

Elliott raised his eyes.

'I found them just after these,' Ben said.

With a sense of dread, Elliott turned to face him. 'Why didn't you tell me about the new pages before? Why didn't you just add them together?'

'Dunno.' Ben shrugged. 'Forgot, I suppose.'

'What do you mean, you forgot?'

'I don't know, all right?' Ben said, matching Elliott's growl. 'Look, I can't remember where I found them, OK? Do you want to read them or not?'

Elliott saw from Ben's expression that he genuinely couldn't recall where he had found the latest set of diary pages. He watched anxiously as Ben reached into his jeans pocket for the four sheets of paper. 'I put them here,' he said. 'To make sure I didn't lose them,' he added, as if that made perfect sense.

Are we being fed this diary in dribs and drabs? Elliott wondered. Not finding it accidentally, but being *given* it to read in pieces? If so, why?

'That's all I have,' Ben said, handing the sheets over.

Elliott felt a shiver leap through him as he studied Ben's calm, relaxed face. Then he opened the first crumpled page.

30th November. I've spent the week trying to persuade Mum and Dad to leave. I've started a nightly rant about it, and even though Mum likes it here, and seems almost as much in love with the portraits as Eve was, she's weakening. The trouble is that Eve seems completely fine again. She's behaving perfectly. No more following the portraits in a merry-go-round the house. But after what Janey told me, I'm more worried than before. I found a damaged portrait hidden away on the fourth floor earlier today as well. It's a horrible study of a teenage boy in muddy boots with a slash through the middle of his head.

'It's Sam,' Janey told me, when I asked her about it.

'You cut it, didn't you?' I said.

'Yes.'

'Why?'

'Because Sam told me to. He doesn't want people to see the look of fear on his face. That's what *Cullayn* wants.'

5th December. After all the scariness of the last few weeks, today was different. Janey came hopping into the garden as excited as a puppy. She was dying to show me something.

'Come here,' she said, laughing as she dragged me to the entrance of the East Wing. 'Watch. A trick the ghost children showed me.'

Lifting her left hand, she slowly splayed her fingers. For a moment nothing happened. Then the air spluttered and crackled around her fingertips. 'Keep watching,' she said. 'That's not it.' Steadying herself, holding her arm away from her body, she reached forward and thrust two fingers inside the East Wing.

As soon as they pierced the stale, dry air there was a faint apricot gleam. 'See?' she said. 'I'm finding a way in. Cullayn's hiding in the dark of the East Wing. No torch is going to find him the way he cloaks himself. But this' – she *clicked* her fingers, and with each click the light expanded – 'gets into his corners, shows me where he is.'

Her hand stirred the air like a spoon. 'Cullayn's not like us,' she said. 'He can dissolve himself, slip like dust into the pores of walls. Or do the opposite, make a solid form, like a fist.' She laughed, made a fist of her own and spread her fingers to swirl the air. Then she grunted 'Ouch!' as her apricot light was abruptly snuffed out.

She yanked her hand back. 'Mm,' she mused. 'Cullayn doesn't like me invading his little kingdom. Good. I don't care. I'm going after him. Someone has to.'

'What are you thinking of doing?' I asked.

'I'm not sure yet. But what do you reckon to this?' She gave me a mischievous smile. 'Alice taught me this trick. I can use it to stop Cullayn, or at least slow him down if I get close enough.'

Janey swung her wrist lazily back and forth inside the East Wing. She looked like she was casually summoning a servant. 'I'm fishing,' she said, grinning. 'Casting a line. Let's see what's there, shall we? See if we can attract his attention ...'

At first nothing happened. But Janey kept at it, flicking her fingertips until her wrist suddenly jolted.

'Whoa!' she said, and I could see she was surprised. 'I guess I hooked something!'

'Hey,' I said, concerned for her.

'It's all right,' she told me. But her eyes widened as she tried to withdraw her hand and found she couldn't.

'Janey,' I said, moving closer to her. 'Tell me how to help.'

'It's OK,' she answered testily. 'I'm fine. If I can just get my hand out again ...' She grinned fiercely. 'It's Cullayn himself, casting his *own* net,' she said. 'If I just keep doing this, I'll be ... I'm sure I'll be OK ...'

I think Janey was trying to impress me with a show of bravery, but of course Cullayn didn't care about that. And while she kept tugging, pushing out her slim fingers, gripping and ungripping, the owner of Glebe House reached out for her. It was terrifying what I saw next, and not only because it was the first time I'd seen Cullayn, but because it happened so *fast*.

A gap came first. It flashed open in the air between Janey's shoulder and her uplifted arm. Then, from the rip of air, a thickly-haired male forearm tore itself from some kind of no-space between the realms of life and death. The owner seized Janey's arm. Two shades of light sparked, competing: Janey's apricot hue, and Cullayn's dark orange-red light. Where they crossed the light curdled into a dirty yellow, but Cullayn's light was stronger, and so was his grip, and he started to draw Janey inside.

Janey fought him. She didn't really know what she was doing, I could see that, but for a moment her sheer determination to stand her ground against Cullayn kept him back: her considerable will opposing his.

But it wasn't enough, and only two things enabled her to break away. First, I threw myself into her, knocking her down. Second – and I think this was more important – another light appeared, a blaze of blue, and I heard a gruff man's voice bellow in pain as the blueness stabbed into Cullayn's wrist, making him let go. For a moment the face of a boy – Sam's face – appeared in that fog of blue, and he was looking not at me but at Janey.

'I know, I know,' Janey muttered to Sam from the floor. 'I need to be more careful. Yes, yes. I know!'

Muttering to herself, she led me back into the garden, holding her wrist. 'I'm OK,' she said, when I tried to look at it.

'You're not OK,' I told her. 'Cullayn was dragging

you into the East Wing! If Sam and I hadn't been there ...'

'It wasn't ... quite what I expected,' she admitted, cursing under her breath. 'I'll be more careful in future. But what you don't understand is that if I go in the East Wing I won't be alone. You saw the way Sam follows me everywhere. The ghost children just need a bit of a push. I'm sure they'll follow me inside if I go after Cullayn. And against all of us I don't think he stands a chance.' She smiled tensely. 'He's only one to our five, Theo. And then, once he's gone ... well, something wonderful might happen.'

'What do you mean, wonderful?'

She folded her arms under her chest. 'The ghost children will be able to leave. They're only staying here because of Cullayn. They won't leave until he does. That's my dream – to help them reach the other side. If I can get rid of Cullayn, they'll be free to go at last.'

Ever since then Janey has been practising in private for her battle with Cullayn. She won't tell me what she's planning. She says Cullayn may be listening. But in truth I don't think Janey knows herself. She's determined to go through with it, though. I don't know whether to try to stop her or not. She already looks tired.

'That's what Sam says,' she admitted. 'He says I'm not ready to face Cullayn. But don't worry, I won't do anything until I'm prepared.' Her chin hardened. 'Until my will matches his.'

13

A RIVER OF MOONLIGHT

'I've found her!' Dad cried, striding into Ben's bedroom. 'Her full name is Jane Amanda Roberts and she lives locally.'

'She still lives here?' Ben said.

'Yep.' Dad looked pleased with himself. 'In the village itself. Very active in the community, apparently. I couldn't find anyone with a bad word to say about her. And that impression was confirmed when we talked on the phone.'

Elliott gazed up. 'You spoke to her?'

'Surprised, eh? She's ever so quietly spoken. Tiny little voice. Had a neighbour over when I called. Gladys. They were having tea and cakes. Lots of clinking china.' When Elliott looked doubtful, Dad said, 'I know. Doesn't sound much like the girl in Theo's story, eh? But maybe that's because she isn't. She explained the mystery. Says the diary was something she and Theo made up. An elaborate hoax.'

'You believe her?' Elliott asked.

Dad shrugged. 'She was convincing enough. She'd forgotten about the past disappearances in Glebe House, though. Couldn't remember the name of the little girl who used to live here. Said her memory was like a sieve these days.'

Elliott's openly contemptuous expression made Dad raise an eyebrow.

'You think she's lying?'

'Make up your own mind,' Elliott said. 'Read this.'

He handed over the latest fragments of the diary. Dad read them slowly all the way through.

'Still believe it's a hoax?' Elliott asked.

Dad rubbed his chin thoughtfully, his confidence dented. 'I'll admit it's described in more detail than I'd expect. But look, Elliott ...' He hesitated, shook his head. 'If this diary *is* real you're asking me to swallow a whole lot more than the fact that Jane Roberts is lying. There's all this other stuff about ghosts and, frankly ... it might help if I could come up with a single reason why a lady who's been living quietly in the village all this time would lie.'

'Unless she had something to do with it,' Elliott said. 'Unless she was part of the reason Eve disappeared.'

'The elderly woman I talked to didn't sound dangerous.'

'She was younger then, Dad. Plenty strong enough to deal with a seven-year-old girl.'

'But there's nothing in the diary to suggest it, either,' Dad argued. 'If the diary means anything, it's obvious she was trying to *protect* Theo and Eve, not harm them.'

'Maybe things changed,' Elliott said. He didn't even know what he meant by that. He was just reaching out blindly. But the image of Janey as a forgetful tea-and-china-cups lady didn't ring true. He turned to Ben. 'What do you think?'

'What?' Ben shook himself. He'd been staring blankly at the wall all this time.

'You OK?' Dad asked him.

'I'm fine.' Ben smiled, gazed out of the window and back again. He had nothing to add. No opinion on events. Or Janey. Or anything.

Elliott looked at him a moment, then said to Dad, 'What about Glebe House? Did you find out any more details about what happened here?'

'Yes. Some.' Dad wavered. 'I'm really sorry to have to tell you both this, but ... children did go missing here around Theo's time. Two of them.'

'Two?' Elliott glanced up, his pulse rising.

'I know,' Dad said quietly. 'I didn't expect that, either. Not the news any of us wanted to hear. But I didn't only get that from Janey. I rang the post office and the woman who runs it confirmed the children's names: Eve Stark and her brother, Theo.'

Elliott felt like he'd been struck in the face.

'I guess that's the tragedy the current owners didn't want to talk about,' Dad murmured. 'Children disappearing.'

'I think Janey's lying,' Elliott said. 'I think the diary is the truth and that she knows exactly what happened.'

'Maybe,' Dad conceded. 'In any case, I'm not spending any more time here figuring it out. We're leaving tomorrow.'

Ben, for the first time, spluttered into life. 'But why?' he piped up. 'I'm getting used to it here. It's OK. It's fine. I want to stay.'

A cold feeling crept through Elliott. 'When did you start liking it here?'

'I didn't say I liked it,' Ben protested. 'It's just that we can't leave. We need the money, and—'

'We don't need the money that much,' Dad cut him off. He gave Elliott a curious look, then faced Ben. 'Let me worry about things like money, all right? We're getting out. I'm sealing the house back up. Then we're off.'

'But what about Eve?' Ben protested, throwing up his arms. 'We'll be leaving her alone here ...'

Elliott watched him closely. So did Dad.

'Eve won't be forgotten about,' Dad said after a long pause. 'On the way back I'll hand the diary to the police.'

Ben gave a grunt of frustration, kicking the wall.

'It's not fair on Eve!' he yelled. 'It's not! She's been

in the house all this time on her own. We're the first people here in ages, and now ... now we're leaving her all alone again.' He was breathing hard. 'Who knows how long it'll be before anybody else comes? She'll be stuck with nothing to do. I know she's only a ghost but we can't just leave her here on her own, Dad. We can't!'

Elliott said quietly, 'It's interesting that you're not scared of Eve any more, Ben. A few hours ago you were terrified of her. What's changed?'

Ben started to reply, then fell silent, as if anything he said would incriminate him.

After giving Ben another measured look, Dad said, 'I'll contact Eve's surviving family. If she's here somewhere they can decide what to do. But we're definitely not staying. I want both of you packed and ready to leave by twelve o'clock tomorrow, no later.'

Ben protested a little more, but Dad refused to budge, and afterwards he drew Elliott aside. 'I'm going to sleep in the room next to yours tonight,' he told him. 'What shall we do with Ben?'

'Make him stay in my room, where I can keep an eye on him.'

'Agreed,' Dad said.

Ben tried to squirm out of staying with Elliott that night. He kept saying that he was OK, felt fine, wasn't scared, didn't understand what was wrong with everyone. The more Elliott heard, the more convinced he became that Ben was being influenced in some way by the house.

They had a bite to eat with Dad around eight p.m. After that, Ben, still arguing, reluctantly brought a mattress and blankets into Elliott's room from his own bedroom.

Dad set up in the room next door. Earlier, he'd paid special attention to securing the East Wing. Its entrance had been resealed in a way no one could dismantle without specialist tools, whatever patience they might have for the task.

Just after eleven o'clock, with Ben's agreement, Elliott switched off all the lights in the bedroom. Inevitably, as soon as he dropped his head back on his pillow, Elliott started listening for noises in the corridor outside. It was impossible not to.

Ben lay in the darkness, saying not one word.

What happened when you went inside the East Wing earlier? Elliott wondered. Ben was somehow more comfortable in the house since then. How could anyone be *more* comfortable after being inside that place?

'I keep humming Eve's rhymes,' Elliott muttered, looking for a reaction – something, anything – from Ben. 'Can you believe that? I can't get them out of my head.'

'They're pretty crazy rhymes.'

'Yeah.'

More silence. Ben didn't move under his sheets. He was so still that at one point Elliott, pretending to adjust his own pillows, leaned across to make sure he was still there.

Ben's round face gazed blankly back at him.

Details from the diary kept jumping into Elliott's mind. Was it really just a work of fiction? No, he didn't believe that. But then what was Janey hiding? And what had happened to Theo? The more he read, the more Elliott had come to care about the boy in the diary. *My friend*, he thought, realising that he meant it. The possibility that Cullayn had somehow got his hands on him was unbearable.

'What about the rhymes?' he asked Ben. 'What do you think they mean?'

'I haven't got an opinion. Just go to sleep, Elliott.'

'You think each name refers to a person who died? Someone Cullayn killed?'

'Maybe.'

'Do you believe the diary's telling the truth?'

'Maybe.'

'*Maybe*? Is that all you've got to say about anything? When you're not weeping over Eve, that is. When you're not begging and crying to get Dad to stay.'

Normally that would have got an immediate and

incendiary reaction from Ben. Elliott had deliberately jibed him as a test.

Ben just gave a low chuckle. 'Yes, it is all I've got to say. I'm tired. Let's just go to sleep. Nothing's going to happen.'

Elliott turned over in the dark. 'You're confident about that, are you? You can sleep quite happily?'

'Sure,' Ben replied in a reasonable manner that to Elliott sounded totally false. 'Look, we're not alone, are we? Dad's right next door. And if Eve's around, I don't think we should be scared of her. She's just a little girl who wants to play, that's all. We should be feeling sorry for her, not scared. We'll be fine. Don't worry. Eve probably won't visit us tonight. She'll just stay in the East Wing. Let's get some rest.'

Elliott edged across to the left side of his bed and gazed at his brother. A river of moonlight flowed across Ben's face from the window. His motionless hands were outside the covers. He looked like he was waiting very patiently for something. Elliott caught him whispering a couple of words. Then, seeing that he was being watched, Ben fell hushed again.

Elliott remained awake.

So did Ben. An hour or so later, he said irritably, 'It's OK, Elliott. Go to sleep, will you? You're making me nervous. Eve's harmless – just a sad lonely little girl who's been on her own too long.'

'So you're not worried about her coming in to say *hi* tonight?'

'No. I think we're going to be OK. There's two of us.' Ben smiled in the dark. 'Unless you run away, like you said you would if the ghost came. Except you didn't, did you? You stuck close to me when Eve turned up. You looked after me. Thanks, Elliott. I knew . . . I knew you would.'

This compliment was so unlike any conversation Elliott had ever had with Ben before that he didn't bother replying. Instead, he lay tensed and rigid in the dark.

Ben wiped a curl of hair out of his eyes. 'I'm going to sleep now.'

'OK, you do that.'

'Are you all right, Elliott?'

'Yes.'

'Are you going to go to sleep?'

'When I'm ready.'

'When will that be?'

'Soon.'

'Good,' Ben said, and with that he turned onto his side as if everything was settled.

Elliott leaned back against his pillow, gazed straight up at the ceiling and blew out a long breath.

A few minutes later Ben said from the darkness, 'Should we leave the door open? You know, in case she wants to come in?'

'No,' Elliott answered. 'We might be asleep. We don't want it – her – coming in without us knowing about it, do we?'

14

WITH HIS EYES
WIDE OPEN

But Eve came anyway.

With a ghost's patience, she waited on the second floor for everyone to fall asleep. While she waited she spent the time playing with Katerina: dismantling her limbs and screwing them back together again, combing her hair with an old brush and messing it up again. Katerina was always getting her hair in such a tizzy muddle.

Elliott stayed awake for much longer than Cullayn planned, but it didn't matter. He fell asleep in the end.

Once she knew he was fully asleep Eve slipped upstairs. She stole past Dad's room, opened Elliott's door and tiptoed through. She felt much more self-assured than before. The hollows of her eyes were like delicate smudges of charcoal. By the light of the moon her pale face was so white it was almost green.

Ben was asleep, too. Sheer fatigue. He'd tried to stay awake, but he'd been doing a lot of wandering recently and he was tired. Eve watched him avidly. Her small teeth shone. Leaning forward, she dared him to wake. She wanted him to leave the room with his eyes wide open.

Janey Amanda Roberts eased into the room moments later. Her rendezvous with Eve was prearranged. Secret paths led into this place, and Janey knew everything about Glebe House, and had trained herself to avoid unnecessary noise as she padded in and out of spaces.

The ghost of Eve stared at her and Janey stared back. Eve did not blink, but Janey had no choice. Janey knew her place. Not wanting to interfere with what Eve was doing, she bowed her head deferentially, retreating into the room's shadows.

Eve prepared her little-girl pout, puffed out her dead lungs and on a whim blew hard on Ben's cheeks.

He woke with a start, and only the untouch of her hand over his mouth prevented him from crying out.

Eve bent down to his warm earlobe. 'Come with me,' she whispered.

Ben glanced towards the sleeping Elliott.

'No, not him,' Eve said. 'I want to show you something. He won't let us go alone.'

'But—'

'No. Come on. This is just for us. A special thing. Come on.'

When he hesitated, Eve smiled. It was a smile that

said everything would be fine, and because it imitated Cullayn's smile, which had been drawing him to the East Wing for days in a way he could not understand, Ben followed her. The hem of Eve's red dress swirled like a bridesmaid's train against the musty carpet as she ran lightly from the room. Her feet sprayed dust. She was swift, and she trailed an arm behind her, like a mother guiding a child, and Ben put his larger hand around her small one and followed her out.

She led him serenely down the sweeping oak staircase.

The entrance to the East Wing was barricaded. Dad had screwed six sturdy planks of cherry rosewood in a cross-hatch across the entrance. Neither Ben nor any little girl, dead or otherwise, could have stripped them off without waking someone.

Janey, demurely trailing in Ben's footsteps, came forward. She'd already surveyed the house earlier tonight, especially this part. Her own weak wrists were fumbling ducks, but a tool merchant had hired her an electrically-driven bracketed screwdriver which could work efficiently in near silence.

She methodically removed the planks. Ben ignored her presence. He was focused utterly on Eve.

Eve gave Janey a measured glance when she was done. The glance was nothing like a child's. 'If we wait for long enough something wonderful might happen,' she said mockingly in her sing-song voice, repeating Janey's greatest hope for the ghost children.

Janey did not react, but Ben did. Seeing the disharmony of the exchange disturbed the tranquillity of his mood. For the first time he felt slightly nervous. Eve realised that if she didn't recover rapidly, Janey would have to take over, and Daddy would know she'd messed up. She didn't want that, didn't want him not trusting her, so she flung out both hands to Ben like a dancer offering the stage to a partner. She giggled. 'Come on,' she said, impatient, excited. 'Into the lovely quiet and dark.'

Ben let Eve's hands guide him inside. He wasn't quite certain why he was here – was a little confused about why he wasn't asking questions – but Janey helped him, prodding his chin up to the portraits. Seeing them always made things clearer.

Eve kept up a brisk pace. She didn't give Ben much time to think. He accepted that, not even bothering to look far ahead because there was no light to see by. Curiously, the darkness did not seem anywhere near as bad or scary to him as it had before. Stumbling occasionally, he trotted along – trying to keep up with Eve – while Janey, unnoticed, followed behind.

At the next intersection Eve took a tight right turn, slapping the walls as she went. As Ben hurried after her dizzy feelings overcame him. He stopped, looking around. Eve was unexpectedly gone. Her hand, the one which had so recently been holding his, was no longer there.

Ben took a small step forward, suddenly frightened. Ahead of him a scrap of moonlight illuminated the floor.

'Hey!' he called, hearing Eve's voice in the distance. 'Where are you?'

She was somewhere ahead of him, singing rhymes. A few rhymes he already knew. The rest related to dead people he had not heard about before.

'. . . T for Tobias, a swish of the scythe. And also for Tanya, who writhed and writhed. U is for Ursula, dead and drawn, V for Victoria, turfed by dawn . . .'

She's helping me to catch her up, Ben thought, not really listening. It felt like a game.

He ran toward the sounds. Eve stayed just ahead of him, her words blurred by distance. As Ben turned left into a new corridor, he heard '. . . J is for John, once quiet and tall. What happened to John again?' Eve's faraway voice gave a happy squeal. 'Oh yes, he fell from a wall!' Shrieking with laughter she ran on, always staying at the edge of Ben's vision.

Breathlessly he followed, but she was going too fast. He called desperately for her to slow down.

'No, no, come on, hurry!' she demanded, not unkindly, and only when Ben got too tired to keep up did she return to him. Staring at him a moment, she thrust a sketch into his hand. 'Do you like it?' she asked, obviously wanting him to.

Ben could barely see the sketch in the darkness, but he said yes anyway, hoping she'd stay with him.

She did a moment, kissing his hand. Then she was off again, skipping up the corridor. Ben lost sight of her immediately. 'Don't forget to show Elliott the picture,' she murmured, even the sound of her almost gone now.

One final verse came back to Ben, fluttering on her high voice.

> Where's the Ogre?
> Where's he been?
> Where's he hiding, all unseen?

Eve's words died away.

'Eve?' Ben whispered.

But she was no longer with him. Nor was Janey. Janey was never invited this deep inside the East Wing.

Ahead, the corridor descended. At the bottom of that descent was a small set of steps. At the bottom of those steps was a dark passageway.

Folding up and tucking Eve's picture inside his pyjama top pocket, Ben walked cautiously down the steps into the passageway and looked around.

One wall showed the usual portraits of Cullayn. The

owner smiled in three different ways from them.

The other wall was blank, moonlit.

A strangely terrified feeling suddenly swarmed inside Ben. *Time to get out*, part of him thought, the true part, knowing it was important.

Instead he lay down. It was hard not to. It felt good. It felt right.

The carpet in the corridor was crusty with age but not so dust-ridden that Ben couldn't put his cheek against it here, and here, and rest his lips just there, off the surface.

This place felt special. To be so deep inside did not feel wrong. Was that because Eve had made her home here? Was her home now *his* home? That idea should have filled Ben with unimaginable fear, but instead he found himself stretching out his arms and legs. He felt unaccountably drowsy. Why not have a nap? Or a longer sleep? He directed his gaze at the roof. Little swirls of plaster caught the moonlight.

I could live here, he thought. The idea came unbidden into his mind, and it did not feel odd.

It was a statement of victory, but not Ben's.

Behind him, the blank wall slid open.

15

UNFED FOR SO LONG

Later that night the moon rose higher in the night sky, seen by some, not by others.

Janey stood near the East Wing, resting against a wall. She was out of breath. It had been difficult carrying the sleeping Ben back to Elliott's room, and then having to drag herself all the way downstairs again to refit the planks over the East Wing entrance. The metal screws had taken a lot of work. And, of course, when it was Elliott's turn to go inside, she would have to open it again.

Eve had surprised her and Cullayn by asking for permission to deal with Elliott herself. She wanted to do it alone. 'A game, Daddy, a game. I won't mess up. I won't! It'll be fun!' She'd hopped and buzzed around Cullayn like a dragonfly until he agreed.

Cullayn had pretended to object, but Janey had seen how secretly pleased he was that Eve was taking the lead. She was his undisclosed weapon, his little huntress in the making. Cullayn had high plans for Eve. He could have swallowed her soul when she died, taken all that energy in one great satisfying gulp, but he'd kept her close instead. Made her an ally in his hunting plans. Tutored her.

No fun if it's too easy when it comes to Elliott, he'd chided her. Surprise me.

Tucking the pneumatic screwdriver back into its plastic container now, Janey left the Glebe House estate. On her way back to the village she glanced up. A night hawk was in a sycamore tree, preening itself after a kill. With a flick of its tail it headed towards the hunting ground. Janey turned to follow it, her eyes coming to rest on the slope and the trees. Their leafy tops swayed in a mild breeze, brightened by moon-gleam and stars.

Only Elliott left now, she thought. One more child to fish out.

Eve didn't need her help any more. The little girl was determined to do it all herself. She had already instructed Ben on what to do tomorrow. He'd remember his part in the morning. Eve was the fisherman now, Ben her shiny lure. Janey wondered what plan the two of them would hatch. It wouldn't be straightforward getting Elliott back inside the East Wing. But then again, if Cullayn had taught the imaginative Eve one thing, it was how to turn everything into a game.

16

THE DOLL'S HOUSE

Elliott couldn't remember falling asleep, and woke next morning from a night of troubled dreams. By contrast, Ben seemed refreshed. Up bright and early to the bathroom he was, washing his face and brushing his teeth until they gleamed. His tiredness was gone. Even his bruise looked less angry.

'I'm starving,' he announced at breakfast, tucking in.

While he ate he chatted perkily about Eve the ghost. He didn't seem to mind sharing a house with her after all. Elliott and Dad had little appetite, but Ben savoured his food. He looked so genuinely unconcerned to be in the house that Dad nearly revised his decision to leave today. Had his judgment been overhasty? No, he decided. We're leaving anyway. He reminded them of the departure time: twelve noon. By then he'd have the razor-wire back over the main gates and the external alarms set. Heading off into the grounds, he left clear instructions with Elliott to remain with Ben at all times and to stay away from the East Wing.

No need to tell Elliott that, of course. He had zero plans to go anywhere near it.

'You've changed your tune,' he said, when he and Ben were back in his bedroom.

Ben was whistling as he put his toothbrush and a couple of shirts into a carry-all. He took his time folding his pyjamas. 'It's OK. We're going. I get it,' he said. 'I'm not happy – I think it's wrong to leave Eve here – but, well, there's nothing I can do about it, is there, so ...' He shrugged.

'What's that?' Elliott said. He'd seen something white poking from Ben's pyjama top – a creased sheet of paper.

'Dunno,' Ben said. He removed the sheet, unfolded it. 'Oh, wow!' With open-mouthed excitement he handed it to Elliott.

The sketch showed a large doll's house. The front of the house had been removed to show five partitioned floors with twelve rooms. Each room was filled with dolls. In front of the doll's house stood Eve. She was holding out a hand in a hopeful way towards a boy standing to her left. The boy was Elliott. On the other side of her, already holding Eve's hand in the sketch, was Ben. The three of them formed a little human daisy-chain. It was a happy-looking picture. A girl with her friends.

Elliott stared at the sketch. 'Me and you and her,' he whispered.

'And a doll's house,' Ben added breathlessly. 'Didn't you say there was a doll's house in the attic?'

'Yes, but—'

'But what?' Ben cried. 'That's it! That's what she's telling us! She *does* want to play! I told you! Come on!'

Before Elliott could stop him, Ben was on his way out of the room.

'Hey, where are you going?' Elliott ran hard after him, but Ben had always been fast, and Elliott only caught up with him on the fifth floor.

The ladder to the attic was inexplicably lowered. Elliott wondered if Dad had been fetching stuff from inside. Ben was already clambering back down the steps, a huge box balanced in his arms.

'See! This is what she wants!' he said. 'She must have come in during the night and put the sketch in my pocket to let me know. She came in when we were asleep, Elliott. She *could* have hurt us, but she didn't. I told you she wasn't dangerous. She only wanted to ask us for help, so she could play with this . . .' Ben studied the box, turning it over. 'It must be too hard for her to fix up on her own,' he said. 'Before we go we have to set it up. Come on!'

'Ben—'

'No, stop arguing! It won't take long if we do it together,' Ben growled. 'What's the matter with you? At least this way she has something to play with after we abandon her.'

Elliott hesitated. He had grave doubts about Eve, but what was the harm in erecting the doll's house? They were already packed to go. It would give Ben something to concentrate on for an hour or so until Dad was ready.

'All right,' he said. 'But that's all we're doing. We'll put it up and then leave it here, OK?'

Ben smiled. 'OK.'

It was a Victorian doll's house. Lovingly packaged, the contents were still wrapped in all their original cardboard boxes. Elliott read the fancy label. *A magnificent home, dignified and grand. A home to delight and grace the play of every girl.*

Ben tapped the box happily. 'Perfect,' he said. 'She's going to love this.'

It took a few minutes to unwrap all the pieces of wood for the structure. Ben laid them out, while Elliott did most of the assembly. Once the roof was ready, they both stood back to assess what they'd built.

'Wow,' Elliott said, genuinely awed by the doll's house's unexpected size.

With the chimney fitted it was over three feet high and two deep. Inside were twelve lavishly furnished rooms. Some of them had textured carpets and pasted-on wallpaper. Surprisingly realistic paper-flames licked the fire-grate in the living room.

'Ha! Check this out!' Ben laughed. He'd found a tiny

toilet with a hinged wooden seat. He waggled it up and down. 'I don't suppose this gets used a lot by the dolls.'

'I guess not.'

The dolls themselves were amazingly life-like. Elliott had expected shiny Cinderella-types. These figurines were much more impressive than that. Crafted out of wood, they were all unique. Each had been individually painted with flesh-tones for the skin, brighter colours for the clothes. There were dolls of boys and girls, but surprisingly most of the figures were men and women, variously dressed. One red-headed woman had been sculpted with a pleated cotton skirt. Something must have gone wrong with the creamy paint used on her skin, though, because it was dark, pitted and flaking.

'You think Eve'll like these?' Elliott asked dubiously, examining them.

'Oh yeah,' Ben said. 'I think she'll like them all.'

Elliott watched as Ben unwrapped items of furniture and placed them in the appropriate rooms. Deeply absorbed, he finished doing that and then grabbed hold of two dolls, unselfconsciously waggling them around.

'Happy now?' Elliott asked. He couldn't help smiling.

'Yeah,' Ben said, giving him a sheepish grin. 'I suppose we're done here. I'm hungry. You?'

'Sure. Let's see what's left in the kitchen.'

Making their way downstairs, they found a bag of

cheese rolls Dad had prepared for the journey, and took a couple.

Dad popped in to check they were OK while they ate. 'We're going in less than an hour,' he told them. 'Make sure you're ready.'

They both nodded.

A few minutes later, Ben gave Elliott an eager look. 'C'mon, let's just check,' he said.

'Check what?'

'If she's playing with the doll's house, stupid.'

'Ben—'

With a hoot, Ben sprang up from his chair, laughing as he beat Elliott to the door. He sprinted up the first staircase.

'Ben, for God's sake!' Elliott yelled, but his brother's laughter just rolled back to him from above.

By the time Elliott reached the fifth floor he was out of breath. The doll's house stood exactly where they'd left it in the corridor.

'See?' Elliott said, annoyed. 'She hasn't found it yet. Come on. That's enough. Let's go.'

'She *has* found it,' Ben whispered. 'Look. The dolls have been moved.'

At first Elliott couldn't see what Ben meant. Then he noticed a straggly blonde-haired doll lying face down at the bottom of some steps.

'*A is for Alice, who fell down the stairs,*' Ben murmured.

'Remember the verse? We didn't leave her like that.'

Elliott felt his pulse race as he reached for the doll of a young boy. With a bright blue cape draped across his shoulders, the boy lay face-down in a posture of exhaustion.

'*L is for Leo, who gave his all,*' Ben whispered. 'Remember him? Remember what he was wearing when Cullayn sent him up the slope?'

Elliott spotted the red-headed doll with the flaking skin. Her head had been rammed up against the paper-flames of the fireplace.

'*S is for Sandra, burning bright,*' Ben said.

Elliott's nerves twitched. 'How come you remember the rhymes so well?'

Ben shrugged. 'Catchy, I guess. Hold on. What's this?'

A hole, filled with water, had been dug into the grounds of the house. The figure of a man, trying to claw his way out, was arranged inside.

'*O is for Oliver, who splashed till he sank,*' Ben muttered.

'I don't remember that verse,' Elliott said.

Several dolls were in bizarre places. Elliott didn't want to look too closely, though he sensed they all related to the rhymes. Which meant, of course, that Eve almost certainly *had* played with the doll's house before. And then Elliott realised it was worse than that. These dolls didn't belong to the original doll's house at all. Eve must have made them herself. Must have whittled away endlessly at the wood and painted them by hand. And where had she got the descriptions of the dead people from? Only one man knew those details. He must have been perched on her shoulder for hours to achieve individual likenesses like this . . .

With terror rising inside him, Elliott whispered, 'Let's go.'

Ben didn't resist when Elliott grabbed his arm, but only because there was no need.

A shadow had spread across the wall behind him.

Eve stood inside that shadow. As straight and still as one of the dolls, she was waiting at the end of the corridor, utterly calm.

Disregarding Elliott, she came swiftly forward. Her eyes were glued to the doll's house. 'You stay here,' she ordered Katerina, unceremoniously dumping her on the floor. Then she changed her mind, picked Katerina up again, and offered her head-first to Elliott. 'To play with,' she explained, when he didn't immediately understand. 'Don't you want to play?'

She grinned, and so did Ben.

While Elliott tried to come up with some kind of reply, Ben said smoothly, 'I'll play,' lifted Katerina and rocked her like a baby in his arms.

'Not like that,' Eve giggled, suddenly very girl-like,

amused at the overly precious way Ben was carrying Katerina.

'Do you like the house we built?' he asked. 'We made it especially for you.'

'Ben, we need to get out of here,' Elliott said.

Ben ignored him.

Eve circled the doll's house a few times, glowing with happiness. With great care she reached out towards the roof. 'May I?' she asked, and Elliott realised that she was asking for permission to touch it. Was that amusement in her voice?

When Ben smiled and nodded, Eve fetched up a man-doll with frizzy black hair and made *clop-clop* noises. 'G is for Guy, crushed under a horse,' she said. She stroked the pale white limbs of a woman. 'J is for Jane, now ageless and white, and also . . .' she threw another doll hard against the nearest wall '. . . for Jack at the end of his fight.'

Standing on her tiptoes, Eve placed a tall man on the roof, then spilled him off. 'K is for blah, blah, blah, blah, blah . . .' Laughing, she snatched Katerina back from Ben, walking her stiff plastic legs robotically towards the doll's house.

Elliott tugged at Ben's arm. He whispered to *just come*.

Ben resisted, hissed back, 'Not yet. We can find out

things. Stay a minute.' He pulled away from Elliott. 'And who are you?' he asked Katerina, touching her plastic cheek. 'A friend?'

Eve nodded vehemently, twisting Katerina's face this way and that.

Elliott tried to work out if he could drag Ben down the stairs. It wouldn't be easy if Ben resisted.

'Ask a question,' Ben said to him. 'Then I'll come with you.'

'My name's Elliott.' Elliott looked straight at Eve. 'And this is my brother.' Eve giggled. 'We're a family who moved in recently, and—'

'This is Katerina,' Eve interrupted him. 'She can't talk. She can only do this.' Eve made Katerina curtsey.

'What about your own brother?' Elliott said, seeing an opportunity. 'What about Theo?' He kept his tone light. 'And your Mum and Dad? Where are they? What happened to them?'

'Oh, I don't know,' Eve said, looking disinterested. Then she gave Elliott a crafty smile. 'Yes, I do! I *do* know! I do!'

She retreated to the staircase. 'Come and find out,' she said. 'Come and I'll show you.'

'Follow her,' Ben whispered.

Elliott did so warily, but only as far as the landing. 'No,' he said. 'We're not going any further.'

Eve glanced uncertainly up at one of the portraits of Cullayn on the wall, then retreated a few more steps. Ben attempted to follow, but Elliott caught his arm. 'No.'

Ben said to Eve, 'It's OK, don't mind him. Have you lost your mummy? I haven't got a mum, either. We're here on our own, just like you.'

Eve's face instantly transformed into one of amusement. She came up to Ben and arranged a small arm around his shoulders. 'Ah, you've lost your mummy,' she said. 'That's bad. Children die in this house, you know.'

'What happened to you, Eve?' Elliott asked.

'I've got to go now,' she told him. 'Daddy wants me back.'

'Who's Daddy?'

'He's right here.' She stared behind her, into the corridor depths.

With his heart racing, Elliott looked where Eve looked. He saw only emptiness.

'He's very close,' Eve insisted. 'I've got to go now or he'll get mad.' Then, with eyes shining in sudden delight, she ran fast towards Ben, shot out her hand and yanked him away with her.

'Hey!' Ben shouted as she hauled him down the staircase.

Eve dug her nails into his arm to make him squeal.

Then, throwing her chin back, she laughed and – flicking a challenging glance at Elliott – ran on with Ben, scurrying fast down one flight of stairs after another. Elliott ran after her, barely able to keep up.

Eve raced across the hall towards the East Wing, pulling Ben along. His feet slid across the marble floor like a mishandled rag doll.

The entrance to the East Wing was open again. Janey Roberts stood next to it. She was holding a screwdriver. When Elliott stopped to stare at her in disbelief, she offered him a terse nod of acknowledgement, then moved aside to let Eve and the protesting Ben go past.

Eve gave Ben a little kiss on the cheek and dragged him into the East Wing.

Elliott hesitated, watching Janey depart through a door leading to the library. Then, hearing a muffled shriek from Ben, he yelled 'Dad!' at the top of his voice and ran inside the East Wing.

17

THE DRIFT OF
CORRIDORS

Eve had a ferocious grip on Ben's arm, and with a swing of her heels she turned left, dragging him with her.

'What are you doing?' Elliott bellowed. 'Leave him alone!'

By the time he reached the same bend in the corridor both Eve and Ben were gone. Then he spotted the flash of Eve's blonde hair bouncing against her shoulders at an intersection ahead. Elliott raced towards her, then stopped when he realised that Eve had led him a few more critical steps inside the East Wing.

'Ben!' he screamed, determined not to get lost. 'Where are you? Shout if you can hear me!"

No answer. Realising the only option that made sense was to find Dad so that they could search for Ben together, Elliott retraced his steps. Or thought he did. Although he'd only made four or five switches of direction he had misremembered one turn. That was enough. One incorrect decision led to three others, and moments later he arrived at one of the dreaded four-way intersections. From here, of course, he could go straight ahead, left or right. Or, if he wanted, he could always go back.

With a shudder of foreboding tearing through him, Elliott came to a crashing halt. He couldn't believe he was back in this place, facing the same numbing choices.

Had Dad heard his shout? Unless he'd been close, it was unlikely.

It's OK, Elliott reassured himself, forcing himself to breathe slowly. Don't panic like last time. Even if you're lost, you can look for Ben.

Calling out Ben's name, Elliott strode down the corridors. He went past endless portraits. Ironic smiles played across the owner's lips.

Two can play at that game, Elliott thought. He started knocking portraits off the walls. When that got no response he smashed the frames underfoot as well, burying his heel in all the faces of Vincent Cullayn. 'Come on, show yourself!' Elliott raged.

Then his foot crunched against something. An expanse of paper lay under his shoes. Even in the dim corridor Elliott could tell it was one of Eve's trademark sketches.

Picking it up with both hands, he spread the paper out.

In the sketch he was standing on the carpet holding the sketch, just as he was in fact doing now. Eve was behind him in the sketch as well, and Elliott couldn't resist looking over his shoulder to check she wasn't there. Relieved that the corridor was empty, he turned back to the sketch, squinting to make out the details.

And saw something behind Eve – something that was too large to be Ben.

Throwing the sketch down, Elliott twisted around, expecting to be attacked.

When he couldn't see anyone he moved on warily.

Five minutes of walking and calling out for Ben later, Elliott decided to try a room. It hadn't worked the last time he was in the East Wing, but the doors couldn't *all* lead nowhere. He picked the nearest one. It led into a bathroom. The room looked innocent enough, and Elliott walked inside. At the back end of the bathroom there was a large circular mirror. Elliott ignored it, leaving the room via the door at its rear.

He found himself in another corridor. A few corridors later he tried a different door. It led into a bathroom with a large circular mirror.

The *same* room as before?

It couldn't be, could it? Cold terror filtered through Elliott at the prospect that he was simply going in circles. He couldn't afford to do that. To make sure he'd know if he entered the bathroom again, he used his finger to mark a big cross in the dust coating the mirror. Dozens of corridors later, hoarse from calling Ben's name, he randomly entered another room.

It was a bathroom. A bathroom with a large circular mirror.

With the sense of being on top of a dam that was about to break, Elliott made himself walk up to the glass.

There, in the mirror, was a shakily-written cross. *His* cross.

But words which hadn't been there before were also written on the mirror. Elliott had to get extremely close to the glass to read them. The tight, angular style was not one he recognised:

Turn your eyes
Upon this dark glass
And see not yourself,
But me

With a yawning dread, Elliott lifted his gaze from the words and refocused on the image reflected in the mirror. Until a moment ago he was sure the glass had only shown the outline of the door behind him. Now the entire mirror was one shifting, trembling weight of darkness. Something stood at the centre of that darkness, watching him.

Elliott automatically raised his fists to protect himself, and turned.

The room was empty.

Shuddering, Elliott felt his entire world starting to dislocate. The only thing holding him together was the fact that he knew Ben was still inside the East Wing, and he had to find him.

Staggering on, he came to a wall. It was covered in a dark scrawl of fresh black ink.

Pick your weapon! Pick your piece!

Elliott had no idea what the words meant and ignored them, heading into the next corridor. He stopped when he saw what was inside.

Weapons. Dozens of them.

Each weapon was laid out on a section of velvet cloth. Many were ancient hunting pieces Elliott recognised from the portraits. Flintlock pistols. Grappling hooks. Snares. Various knives. The items were not heaped together in a pile, but arranged and spread out so that he could see them clearly. To encourage me to choose, Elliott realised.

Curiously, many of the weapons looked as if they might comfortably fit his hand. A long-poled staff. A bludgeon. A brass mesh packed with hooks.

His eyes were drawn to a spiked mace, held inside a

metal-studded glove. Elliott was deeply tempted to try the glove on. A whip also lay within tantalisingly easy reach. So did a length of rope. The rope was already knotted into a noose, as if only waiting for the right-sized neck.

At the end of the display of weapons a message had been stuck on the tip of a narrow-bladed cutlass. Reading it, Elliott had no doubt that it was not Eve but the East Wing's master himself who had left it for him.

Pick your weapon, mister!
Pick your piece!
Garland your limbs
From my gutting-feast

Elliott shivered. An invitation, he realised. An offer to take what he wanted. As many weapons as he liked. And a strange compulsion almost led him to do just that, to load his shoulders with everything he could carry. Elliott had no idea where that compulsion came from, but he felt it luring him in as he plucked up a knife. He tested its weight. He'd never thrown a knife before, but suddenly he had a strong urge to do so, to snatch up the blade by the hilt and hurl it at the nearest wall.

He stopped himself just in time.

No, his instinct told him. Don't. As soon as you accept

the call to arms, that's when the real hunt begins.

Was Eve part of that hunt? Maybe. Elliott no longer doubted that she was working alongside the owner, just as Janey was. But what about Ben? He'd obviously planned the whole play-with-a-doll's-house game with Eve. Did that mean that Ben, like Janey, was now his enemy as well? It didn't matter, Elliott decided. It didn't matter because even if Ben did help Eve, he wasn't responsible. Cullayn was behind everything.

I've still got to find Ben and get him out of here, Elliott realised. I've got to.

On a whim he spat at one of the portraits, just as Janey had done in the diary. No reaction came, or so he thought. The reaction was on its way. It was only moments from arriving.

'I won't pick a weapon!' Elliott snarled. 'I won't do it!'

As if Cullayn had already known he would choose nothing, Elliott came across another note, seared into the wall this time:

Every weapon you do not choose will be used against you and those you love

A moment later, a sliding sound made Elliott glance up.

Ben was waiting ahead of him, at a bend in the corridor.

Gasping with a mixture of fear and relief, Elliott headed towards him. It was only as he strode forward that he realised Ben wasn't waiting to be rescued. One of Ben's feet was pressed against the wall, ready to push off. His other foot was toe-forward in the same way Elliott had seen from Cullayn in so many of the portraits – inviting the chase.

As Elliott yelled out his brother's name, Ben laughed at him.

Then somebody or something – some great arm that was not Eve's – snatched Ben away again, leaving the corridor vacant.

'Not yet,' said a lively voice.

Elliott staggered up the corridor, then came to another crashing halt.

Ahead, the floor descended. There it was: the small set of steps, and, beyond it, the dark passageway.

Elliott's heart tightened. Before he'd had no idea why this area terrified him so much. Now he knew the reason. One wall in the passageway was blank. No doors. No pictures. Cullayn's secret room was here. Was this where the master of Glebe House was hiding?

With his scalp crawling with fear, Elliott stumbled away. Several turns later he found the floor again descending towards a set of small steps ...

Seeing the dark passageway this time, Elliott felt as if he was on the verge of having the most terrifying thought in the world, but he wasn't quite having it yet. He hurried on, bearing mostly left. He only stopped again when the floor descended. Ahead of him was a set of small steps —

This time Elliott thrust his fist into his mouth to hold back a scream.

Keep your eyes shut, he decided. Walk but don't look. Maybe you'll end up somewhere else. But he was too scared to keep that tactic up for long, and when he no longer dared to keep his eyes closed he found himself inside a corridor descending towards a set of small steps . . .

This time Elliott screamed out loud. He couldn't hold it in, didn't even try.

And he ran. It didn't matter where. A shriek of pure terror followed, accompanied by the sound of pounding feet. Both belonged to him. The rhymes of the ghost children's names – Nell, Leo, Alice, Sam – ran like a litany through his head, emerging out of his mouth in one unstoppably grotesque shriek.

Only exhaustion slowed Elliott down. Even that didn't do so for long. As soon as he could, he picked his feet up again and raced on, crashing ahead, the corridors blurring around him, the pictures on the walls all merging into one of the happy owner hunting a terrified boy up a tree-lined slope. Finally Elliott literally *roared* with fear, and that roar – the sheer surprise of it – sent a new slice of terror sizzling through him. But the sound of it also seemed to clear his head, and he realised that he could hear something new.

A thump – and a voice.

Elliott's senses, already tautened to an electrifying pitch, made him scream when he heard it. He would have screamed at anything in that moment, and he screamed again when light flickered in blue-white beams in the corridor ahead.

Something big was there. Definitely a man. For a moment Elliott was so scared that he didn't recognise the sounds coming from the figure. But abruptly the shape widened and someone was there who knew him.

Dad stood inside the East Wing's entrance.

Rushing forward, his long, powerful arms caught Elliott and pulled him to safety.

18

THE OPPOSITE OF CALM

Elliott sank against the strength of Dad's waiting shoulder.

'I'm all right,' he gasped, not caring what he looked or sounded like. 'But Ben's in there. Dad, he's *still* in there!'

Elliott was shaking so much he could hardly get the words out. He stuttered an explanation of the way Eve had dragged Ben into the East Wing. Dad was even more disturbed when Elliott described the change in Ben's own behaviour – the way he'd helped Eve set up the whole episode with the doll's house.

Even in his own frantic state, Elliott could see how bewildered Dad was, how hard it was for him to come to terms with the true horror lurking inside the East Wing. But Dad was beginning to understand, to grasp it, and he'd have run straight in to find Ben if Elliott hadn't stopped him by saying, 'What's that?'

Out of the corner of his eye he'd spotted five sheets

of paper. They were haphazardly flung across the East Wing's entrance.

'Those weren't there before,' he told Dad, recognising the age-curled edges at once. 'It's another part of the diary.'

'You sure?' Dad ran across, studied the writing, saw it was Theo's. 'So we've been left another *instalment*,' he growled, shaking his head. 'No,' he decided, throwing the sheets down. 'No. I'm not wasting time on the diary right now.' He headed towards the East Wing entrance.

'Wait,' Elliott said.

'Wait for what?' Dad demanded, aching to get to Ben.

'We need to know what's in the East Wing.'

'We already know enough, Elliott!'

'No, we don't.'

'We can't just stand here talking!' Dad shouted. 'We've got to get Ben out. This is wasting time—'

'Time is all there is in there,' Elliott whispered, and something about the way he said it made Dad hesitate. 'Let's read the diary before we go in,' Elliott pleaded with him. 'Even if we're together inside the East Wing, I don't think we'll ever find Ben unless Cullayn wants us to. The key to what's going on is in the diary, I'm sure of it. We need to understand that before we do anything else.'

Dad dragged his hands through his hair. Elliott saw

how much he was itching to reject any arguments and get inside the East Wing.

'But isn't the diary itself just one of Cullayn's games?' Dad groaned. 'How do we know he isn't feeding it to us in chunks as a diversion? Games within games. Playing with us. Scaring us.'

'To get us to rush in after Ben?' Elliott said.

'Yes.'

'Then it's working, isn't it?' Elliott noted. 'You're about to go in. You haven't got a clue what you're up against, but you're going to run in there anyway. I bet *that's* what Cullayn wants. I bet he can't wait.'

Dad wavered. 'All right,' he murmured at last, physically holding himself back. 'I'm listening. You think this diary might be ... what? Someone trying to help us? Using the diary as a warning?'

'It could be.'

'But why give us the diary in pieces? It doesn't make sense.'

'I don't know why, Dad. But someone *is* doing it deliberately. You were surprised you hadn't spotted the first part of the diary on that chair in the library, remember? It was obviously left for you. The other parts were left in places for me and Ben to find. Now this piece turns up. It can't be a coincidence. Without help I don't think we're ever going to find Ben in there,' Elliott said firmly. 'I've been inside. So have you. I don't think Cullayn's even trying yet. He's just starting his hunt. There's worse to come.'

'And you think the diary will tell us what to expect?'

'Maybe.'

'But how can we rely on it?' Dad howled, shaking the paper. 'Oh, come on then, quick, quick . . .' With a grunt of frustration, he ran back to Elliott. Propping himself against a wall, he arranged the diary sheets in order. 'It's OK,' he said softly, seeing that Elliott was still exhausted. 'Let's just read it together.'

19th December. Janey was on the couch in the living room when I came downstairs today. Gazing at her more closely, I was shocked to see that she was having trouble sitting up. 'It's OK,' she mumbled, shaking so hard she could barely get the words out. 'I'm . . . I'm dealing with it. Trying to. Only . . . he's got his hooks in me now, hasn't he?' She giggled, a scary sound. '*I went in,*' she said.

She clutched at her dress, not noticing the flower petals falling at her feet.

'That was brave of me, wasn't it, Theo, don't you think?' she murmured, grinning crookedly. 'I woke up and decided to go straight into the East Wing. No more waiting. Just stuck my chin out and went right up to say hi to Vincent Cullayn. And you know something? It all went according to my plan. I got inside. He let me, of course, but I didn't know that then. And the ghost children came with me as well. They followed me in. But not all the way.'

'They left you with him?' I said, appalled.

'Oh yes.' She smiled weakly. 'He and I, alone. The hunter and the hunted.'

I couldn't get another word out of Janey, but later I almost forgot about her because of what happened with Eve. I'd heard a noise coming from her bedroom in the afternoon, and found her casually booting Katerina across the floorboards and mumbling stuff. Thinking she must have a fever, Mum got her straight to bed and called for a doctor. She stayed with her until about midnight, then left a bedside lamp on so Eve wouldn't be scared if she woke.

Hearing whispered rhymes from her room at about 1.00 a.m., I crept in. The first thing Eve did when she saw me was to switch the lamp off. There was a sort of rustling after that. Jumping for the lamp, I got it on in time to see Eve mussing her hair, getting dust out of it. When I saw her, she gave up trying to hide where she'd been and stared defiantly at me. 'I'm going back in again as well,' she told me. 'Whenever I want to. Whenever I want to!'

Then she smiled. I'd never seen that kind of smile

from her before, and I knew it wasn't Eve talking next.

'She's pretty, isn't she?' she purred. 'Janey, I mean. You like her, don't you, Theo? You *really* like her. What do you do? Find yourself smiling at night, thinking about her, wanting to be close to her?'

'Who ... who is talking to me?' I asked, barely able to get the words out.

'Goodnight, Theo,' Eve said, and with a chuckle turned back into her pillow.

*

21st December. Although Janey refused to see me for two days, saying it was unsafe to get anywhere near her, I had to tell her about Eve. Arriving at her house, it was horrible to see the state Janey was in. She'd lost weight and her hair was unwashed.

Seeing my anxious expression, she smiled, but it wasn't a real smile. She stood up calmly to face me, but somehow I knew it was the opposite of calm she was feeling. Then she laughed, knowing the pretence wasn't working, and led me to her room. She tried to talk. Couldn't. She looked so vulnerable in that moment, but refused to let me get any closer.

'It's Eve, isn't it?' she said. 'That's why you're here.'

I could see how hard it was for her to ask. Because depending on what I said she might have to do something, and you could see she wasn't ready for that. She wasn't ready for anything. When I told her what Eve had said to me, Janey's hands grasped the mattress.

'Cullayn knew my weaknesses, Theo,' she whispered at last, breathing in a quiet, desperate sort of way. 'He knew me better than I know myself. I thought I could show the others what might be done.'

'And the ghost children left you in there,' I said. 'They betrayed you.'

'No, you don't understand,' she murmured. 'It was *me* who had a failure of nerve. They didn't follow me in because they knew I wasn't ready. Sam, especially, tried to hold me back. I went in anyway. Couldn't do anything when I saw Cullayn.' She smiled faintly. 'Too scared. Girl here lost her nerve. All gone wrong.'

I walked across to her. Janey held back a moment, then leaned into me.

'You know,' she murmured hopelessly into my shoulder, 'I think Cullayn liked the idea of me trying to hunt him down. He hasn't had fun like

that in ages. But, see, when I reached him and my
first trick didn't work I had no idea what to do
next. I'd never seen him fight. I didn't know what
he could do. I wasn't ready. *But he was.*

'He came after me, Theo. He came after me, and
he was like a storm, and I ran and I ran but
I couldn't get out. He's strong. Stronger than you.
Stronger than me. I should have listened to Sam.
Five minutes Cullayn gave me. "Five minutes to
midnight," he said. That's all it took to shake me
to pieces. He told me I would die in there. But he
was lying. He let me go. Do you know why?' Her
eyes blazed as she turned towards me. 'Because
he wants me alive. I'm more useful to him alive,
see? Cullayn wants me out here in the world,
helping him. An extension of his will. Oh, he'd
love to have me at his bidding. He'd love that.'

Janey dragged her nails across her face. 'I should
have *sneaked* in there,' she said. 'I should have
watched how he moved, seen how to fight by
studying him, instead of announcing myself like a
little toy to be played with.

'Don't you understand?' she raged, fighting me
off when I held her hands to stop her hurting
herself. 'He *got to me*, Theo. There's a bathroom
in the East Wing. Everything leads you to it. It has
a round mirror. When you go in there, Cullayn's

waiting. He's in the glass. It's what he likes to show you just before he begins the hunt for real. And I saw him. And now I can't stop seeing him.'

She scrunched up her hair. 'I was too open. I should've been shutting him out instead of letting him in. He's in the East Wing, but ...' Janey balled her fists, shrieked '... he's dug into me now as well. You can't trust me any more. Don't you see, Theo? He's inside me.' She jabbed her chest. '*In here!*'

I stared into her hollow eyes.

'He's taken a chunk out of me,' she choked. 'I've given him something. I don't even know what it is he's taken from me, but he can do more than just whisper now. I've given him *real strength*. It's someone like me he's been waiting for all this time. And he's using that strength. He wants everything, Theo. He wants to collect more children in there. He wants more and more power. Enough to leave Glebe House. To get out into the rest of the world. Absolute creative power to hunt wherever he pleases.'

Janey couldn't stop shaking.

'The ghost children warned me,' she said miserably. 'They told me not to get too close to him. They kept saying it. But no, that wasn't good enough for me, was it? I had to have a looksee,

156

didn't I? I wanted to get a good look at the legendary Cullayn for myself. And instead he looked at me. And that was that.'

'What are you going to do?' I asked, still holding her.

She glanced at her trembling hands. 'Don't know. Nothing. Don't know. There's a thing, one thing. If I've got the guts to try it. Probably not.' She grinned brokenly. 'It's my fault what's happening to Eve, you know. All the time I've been in Glebe House, Cullayn's somehow been using my gift to strengthen himself. I didn't know, Theo. I didn't! I should never have come into the house. But he wanted me to, he encouraged me – of course he did. He was always waiting to use me.'

She suddenly slapped my hand away. 'No! Why are you so close? Get away! I'm not safe. Stay away from me!'

'I trust you,' I told her.

She laughed bitterly. 'Don't you get it? It's not just me you can't trust. If you stay here, you can't trust *yourself*. He'll use you too if he can, Theo. He'll use Eve and he'll use you. You've got to leave Glebe House now. You've got to convince your parents.'

Janey staggered to the window. I saw winds stir. I sensed it was the ghost children, crowding the glass, trying to support her, and at first I thought Janey wouldn't let them. But out of some instinct to survive she did, pushing the window wide and almost throwing herself out, but instead letting them in, letting the children catch her and hold her up.

*

24th December. Nearly Christmas, but we're not celebrating. Janey warned me that Cullayn had got inside her when she was in the East Wing, but I refused to believe he could control her until today.

It was Mum who spotted Eve walking on top of the fence overlooking part of the lake. The fence is about ten feet high but only four inches wide. If she fell on our side she'd probably be OK. If she fell on the lake-side, she was bound to hit the sharp rocks in the shallows under the ice.

I could see that Eve didn't want to be out there. She was crying. And directly on her heels, walking behind her, equally terrified, was Janey. I knew at once that it must be one of the games Janey said Cullayn was so fond of. Neither girl was in charge of whether they would fall. Would they? Wouldn't they? A game. Cullayn was in control.

Janey was barefoot behind Eve. Sobbing with fear, she was concentrating hard, balancing herself with her arms. In front of her Eve was shrieking, but as long as she kept looking where she was going I thought she'd reach the end of the fence OK and be able to clamber down. Every now and then Janey let one of her hands drift towards Eve, helping to guide her and keep her true.

Mum waited until both of them were safely off the fence before she started shouting at Janey. 'No,' she raged, furious when Janey couldn't explain. 'Janey, how could you? Endangering Eve like that!'

Janey just kept staring tearfully at me, a terrible wounded apology in her eyes. Then with a great howl she ran back home.

'Not one more word with that girl,' Mum said to me. 'I mean it.'

She immediately banned Janey from coming near the house. It was hard for Mum to do that. She's grown so fond of Janey. She's been like a second mum to her, really. A proper mum.

But I couldn't leave it like that. I had to make sure Janey was OK.

Ignoring Mum's order, I went round to her house. I'm looking out of my bedroom window right now, hours later, and I'm still scared to look towards

Janey's place. I don't know what she might be doing in there.

Janey appeared ordinary enough when she let me in. It was only when I was inside her room that I saw the huge portrait of Vincent Cullayn over her bed. She must have stolen it from Glebe House. My heart filled my mouth as Janey turned away from me and stood in front of the portrait. She pressed close up against it. There was a small knife in her right hand. I saw her shoulder tense as she *scratch-scratched* at something in the picture.

I didn't wait for her to finish. I ran towards her. I was trembling. So was she, but with enjoyment. As I approached, she grunted and moved aside.

Cullayn's head was now missing from the portrait. At first I thought that was a good thing – she'd defaced it, damaged it. Good. Then I saw what she'd carved in its place. Knife lines in the shape of her own face. *His* body, *her* face. It could just as easily have been his face, her body. In the painting Janey *was* Cullayn. In the room, Cullayn was Janey.

The portrait showed Cullayn/Janey chasing Alice up the slope. I knew it was Alice because Janey had cut that cruel verse stating her name into the painting. Janey looked happily at the picture. Then she looked at me, as if to say *What do you think of this?* and I'd never been more scared in my life.

I knew it was Cullayn. He was here, inside Janey. The hunter frightening his prey. This time the prey was me. I could see how pleased Janey was to have surprised me. It wasn't her, though, not really. That expression wasn't hers at all. It was *his* protruding lips Janey was mimicking. But I knew then that even if it was only for a while Janey had lost her fight against Cullayn, and I ran from the room.

Janey didn't follow me. She just hissed like a snake. A single word burst through her clenched teeth. 'Eeeeeeeeve.'

*

25th December. Christmas evening. OK. I'm going to record the time because somehow it seems important. It's 8.46p.m., and it's been dark for hours. I'm trembling as I write this, but sitting here outside the East Wing I'm going to make myself record every detail of the hunt, in case anything happens to me. If it does, this diary had better survive, because

The third diary fragment ended on that word *because*. Someone had deliberately torn away the bottom half of the page to hide what was written after it.

Dad shook his head at the final entry, hardly able to contain his fury.

'*Is that it?*' he yelled. 'Is that all we're being offered? Is that meant to be our *help?*' He turned to Elliott. 'One hour. Do you understand? I'm going in there on my own to find Ben and if I'm not back in an hour I want you to ring 999 and tell them there's been a terrible accident. They won't believe a ghost story, but they'll believe that, and you'll get help fast. Do you understand?'

Elliott was barely listening. He'd noticed something.

A sketch had been drawn on the back of the last diary page. It showed Ben standing in an East Wing corridor. His pose was carefree, relaxed. The drawing had definitely been done today as well, because he was wearing the clothes he'd put on this morning. Ben's laid-back attitude in a place as scary as the East Wing was bad enough. Nothing, Elliott knew, could better have shown how much he needed their help. But of course Cullayn liked his games too much for it to be merely a sketch. Clustered tightly around Ben were a series of points. Each had a number next to it. There were eighty-four numbers in all.

As a joke Cullayn had done the sketch in the form of a children's dot-to-dot picture.

Dad found a pencil and rapidly linked the lines between the numbers. When he finished – and saw the grinning bearded figure hidden behind Ben – he immediately ran across to the East Wing. A loose plank of wood lay on the floor outside the entrance. Snapping it across his knee, Dad made a portable weapon with a jagged end. He hefted it.

'One hour,' he rasped. 'If I'm not back make the call.' He hesitated, came back to Elliott, hugged him, snatched a torch from a shelf at the back of the hall, then crashed through the entrance to the East Wing.

*

Elliott watched him set off. Too tall to stand upright, Dad was forced to run bent-over down the entrance corridor. That was bound to be a disadvantage when he got further inside.

Elliott thought of Janey. Nice old lady. Cups of tea. Community-minded. Yeah, yeah. Except they now understood what Cullayn had done to her, didn't they?

Numb with fear, Elliott lowered his face. So the diary had merely been holding out hope to them, only to dash it. Another joke. But Cullayn had also used the diary to inform them of his victory, of course. That was its main purpose. To gloat. Janey had been the brave, gifted girl who'd dared come after Cullayn. Instead, he'd stretched out his eager hunter's arm and grabbed her. How sweet a victory that must have been, Elliott realised. To conquer Janey. Not to kill her, but to enslave her. To master her.

And now Dad was inside the East Wing. Elliott wondered how long it had been since Cullayn crossed wits with an adult? A true hunt that would be. A match, strength on strength. A man.

19

THE LOVELY QUIET
AND DARK

The shadows of the East Wing swallowed Elliott's father whole. They tucked him in darkness. They shrouded his body, pinched him inside and lost him forever.

Dad had no idea what he was facing here, so he did what any decent man would have done in the same situation. He raised his torch. He kept the sharp-edged plank ready. He called out for his son.

'Are you there, Ben?' Then he yelled it: 'Ben! Son! Can you hear me?' And, to make the owner of Glebe House show himself: 'Cullayn! You coward! Is it only children you hunt, then?'

Dad hated naming the owner out loud that way. He sensed that an admission of his power was just what Cullayn wanted – proof that Dad acknowledged him at last. But Dad realised that he had to let the owner know he took his threat seriously if he was to bring him out into the open.

'Give me my boy back or I'll destroy the East Wing,'

he said calmly. 'I'll bring it down. Brick by brick I'll do it. Are you listening to me, Cullayn? I'll destroy your home. I'll hire fifty men and demolish it in a day.'

For a second a booted step thundered menacingly through the East Wing. Then it faded again. *Good*, Dad thought grimly. *At least he's listening.*

The nearest portrait on the wall showed Cullayn hunting a man. The painting brought a tight smile to Dad's lips. Too much time occupied with frightening children, he thought. If Cullayn reckoned pictures like this would scare him maybe he wasn't quite the hunter he believed himself to be.

A coughing noise came from a closed door to his left.

Warily, Dad opened it.

He found himself in a bathroom. At the back of the bathroom was a large circular mirror. Cautiously stepping forward to take a closer look, Dad saw that there was scrubbed-out writing and a large finger-wide *X* on the surface. His own reflection was also caught in the glass. Something else was there, too.

A figure. Crouched. A man as big as he was. Announcing himself.

Dad lifted his weapon in response, but by the time he turned Cullayn had vanished in a low ripple of laughter.

Staring at the wooden shard in his raised hand, Dad had an unnerving sense that he'd passed a critical threshold. By bringing this improvised weapon inside –

and showing that he was prepared to use it – had he somehow brought even more danger to Ben?

Just beyond an intersection point, he heard a child's voice coming from a room. The child sounded like it was crying.

Dad entered the room, holding the plank above his head, ready.

A young person was on the mattress of the bed, hiding under the bedspread. At least it was the size of a child, its head tenting the blankets, and rising as if trying to stand up.

'Ben?' Dad whispered.

'Boys and ploys and toys,' said a voice. It was sing-song, and came from the air all around him.

'Eve?' Dad murmured.

He was still watching the small rising head under the blankets when Eve sighed behind him. With a sharp intake of breath, Dad spun round to face her, but he looked too low – at a girl's height – and she was already mounted on Cullayn's invisible hand.

With a great whip-like crack Eve swiped at his skull.

No ordinary child could have hit him so hard.

Dad fell, spinning, then immediately attempted to get up again. Eve's arm, guided by Cullayn, hit him twice more.

The blows knocked Dad most of the way across the room. Reeling from them, he scrambled upright, his legs buckling under him. The room swam. The torch, which he'd managed to grip all this time, dropped from his hand, landing with a spongy thud on the bedroom carpet.

Dad touched the side of his head. It was slick with blood. The blood flowed freely, but he was far from done. If Cullayn had intended to kill him with Eve's blows, he'd failed.

Staggering around until his head cleared, Dad slowly felt strength return to his legs. He wiped the blood out of his eyes, watching for Eve. She'd vanished as suddenly as she'd appeared. With a bleary stare, Dad found the plank of wood again. Gripped it. Picked up the torch. Surveyed the room. If he had to strike Eve to defend himself would he do it? Yes, he decided. If she gave him no choice. He prepared himself for that.

A child, he thought. *My God, a child! The boys were right.*

Dazed, he stumbled from the bathroom and down another corridor. For several minutes he yelled for Ben, but gradually he slowed. He was weakening. Loss of blood. *Got to find him soon*, he realised. *Before you're too far gone.*

Moments later he came across a message, thickly scrawled on a wall.

What will I do with your sons?

With his heart galloping in fear, Dad stared all around him.

There was no sign of Cullayn. Instead, a piece of paper lay on the floor by his feet. At first Dad thought it was another part of the diary. He was wrong. It was a sketch meant just for him. The sketch was hand-drawn, but the style this time was not at all like Eve's. In the sketch Cullayn was standing at the centre of his hunting ground. He was wearing his leathers and peering around a tree trunk. Hanging off one of his arms was a whip. Hanging off the other arm was a mesh with hooks. Bunched across his shoulders was a coiled whip, a belt stuffed with knives and three or four other weapons Dad couldn't even name.

Elliott and Ben were also in the picture. Elliott was half way up the slope, trying to get away, running his heart out. Ben had already been caught. Cullayn had restrained him with a rope, and was now gazing at Elliott in anticipation of the chase to come.

'Cullayn!' Dad roared. 'Where are you?'

But he suddenly knew that Cullayn was *everywhere*. The owner of Glebe House wasn't restricted to any one part of the East Wing. His presence swirled in the dust and the plaster of the walls. The entire East Wing was his kingdom and manipulation.

Rhymes were being whispered in the closest corridors. Cullayn's essence enlivened them, ramped up their volume. The verses were brought to Dad's ears by two children. He recognised Eve's voice from the higher pitch. He also recognised Ben's.

'Boys and toys and ploys, right and left, round and round his father goes, and down and down . . .'

Dad tried to listen only to Ben's voice. He thought he heard a catch, a hesitation. Then it sounded like Ben was pleading. As Dad lurched to where the voice was coming from, it faded. Moments later he heard it again to his right – again pleading. Twice more Dad heard it. Twice more it faded.

Cullayn's leading me on, he realised. *This is one of his games.*

There was no way Dad could even be certain it was really Ben's voice he was hearing. But how could he walk in any other direction when it might be?

'Wha—'

Abruptly Dad lost his torch, snatched away by a smaller hand.

All around him it was suddenly black. Dad twisted around, bringing his hands up to defend himself.

No attack came, but now he was alone in the dark.

He shuffled his way onward as best he could. Tiny shafts of daylight in the ceiling guided him. Corridors fanned ahead.

And inevitably, of course, he came to one that

descended. That led to a small set of steps. To a dark passageway with a bare, unlit wall.

Without hesitating, Dad took the descending corridor.

He powered down the steps.

'Ben?'

No answer, but the corridor beckoned. As Dad walked inside, the rhymes sung earlier sprang up again. Eve and Ben were hissing them.

'. . . and right and left, and round and round, and down and down . . .'

Dad suddenly wondered how long he had been inside the East Wing. More than an hour? Had Elliott made that call yet?

The dark passage awaited him.

Did he dare walk into the middle of it?

Yes.

As Dad took the first steps his pulse suddenly raced, the hair all over his body standing on end.

'Ben!' he screamed into the darkness. 'Answer me!'

The wall to his left was pale and pictureless, lit up by a sliver of ceiling light. Something about that wall frightened him. The opposite wall was not lit at all. It wasn't logical, but Dad wanted to keep to the darker side of the wall where the portraits were. He was afraid of the lighted, blank wall. The dark wall was scary only because it was dark. The blank wall was scary for a reason he could not understand.

He walked up to the blank wall and felt it. Smooth. It was very smooth. The corridor was quiet and so, the rhymes abruptly ceasing, was Dad.

A strangely terrified feeling fluttered inside him. He couldn't identify the reason for it. Then he realised it was because the worst thing had not yet happened. The worst thing was in one of the sketches Eve had done all those years ago. It was to be hunted down by those you loved.

Moments later Ben stood in front of him. Pushed from a side doorway, he waited only a few metres away, shivering.

As Dad turned towards him, recognising Ben's shape if not his face in the near-dark, something with a long reach thrust from a hidden partition in the blank wall. It was a fist. Covering that fist was a metal-studded glove. The glove clenched a bludgeon – one of the weapons Elliott had failed to pick up earlier. The bludgeon caught Dad with a crushing blow this time, ringing his temple.

Dad clattered to the floor, his legs folding under him.

'Ben,' he murmured, the word barely emerging. And as it died on his lips, Cullayn's voice loudly, impressively, rippled from the darkness.

'Yes, he's here. And, Janey willing, I'll have your other son as well.'

Dad made a huge effort to get up, could not. Feeling himself beginning to lose consciousness, he forced his stinging eyes to focus for a second. Ben and Eve were both standing over him. Neither did anything to help. Ben, though, looked uneasy. That was the only heartening thing Dad could take from the moment, so as he felt himself slipping from consciousness he took it.

He managed to raise his head. There was a shadow behind Eve and his son: a dark veil. It was all hunter.

'Eager spirits and cunning wiles,' Cullayn said, and Dad felt himself roughly lifted, dragged and dumped inside the wall. 'No, don't die yet,' Cullayn growled, standing astride him. 'Remain with us. At least until my Janey brings me Elliott.'

20

A GENTLE GREY LADY

Elliott sat on his haunches outside the East Wing, breathless, waiting for Dad to come out. After watching and listening for an exact hour, he reached for his mobile to dial 999.

Before he had depressed a single digit, Jane Amanda Roberts appeared smoothly at the entrance to the East Wing.

Elliott backed away three steps.

She stood leanly there, old and grey, and he wondered if that was part of her plan: to look helpless. The diary entries had convinced him she was far from that. They had also convinced him that whatever Janey was like before, she was now under Cullayn's sway. Seeing her outside the East Wing with the screwdriver, re-opening the entrance, only made him more certain of that.

Her hands were clasped behind her back. She was holding something. A good hunter keeps its weapons hidden, Elliott thought. Her gaze was all calculation.

'Still pretending to be a weak old lady?' he said, hiding his fear inside a growl.

'Pretending?' she answered serenely back. 'If so, I've got away with it for a long time, haven't I?'

Elliott backed off another step. 'It was you who opened the East Wing when we arrived, wasn't it?'

She nodded.

'You did it so Ben would go inside.'

'Just so.'

Elliott bristled and stood tall, two or three inches above her.

Janey took no notice. 'What do you think I am?' she snarled. 'Something you can defeat with your stature? Your fists? A gentle grey lady, a whiff of bath salts? Is that what you take me for?'

Elliott retreated another step. 'You're the one who spoon-fed us bits of the diary.'

'Of course. Enough to keep you interested. And tiptoeing inside the East Wing, despite yourselves. Exactly. Where are you going, Elliott?' she added. 'Trying to walk away from me already? You haven't finished the diary yet. Is this what you're looking for?'

One of her hands fluttered forward. Clenched inside was a bundle of hand-written pages. Elliott recognised the writing at once.

'The next part of the diary,' he said.

'The final part,' she corrected him.

Elliott swallowed. 'Did you kill Eve?'

No answer. Followed by: 'Perhaps.' And then, as if she was growing bored, or merely tired, Janey took a step sideways. She leaned forward so that her head was inside the East Wing while her wrinkled neck was still in the hall. 'Watch and learn,' she said.

The outline of her hair abruptly crackled with light.

Seeing his chance, Elliott ran. He set off in the opposite direction, through the hall and up the main flight of stairs.

Janey scurried after him. She saw where he'd gone. A bathroom – the one place on the first floor with a working lock on the inside of the door.

She clasped the diary as she came after him. To Janey the words contained in its pages were so full of melancholy that they seemed to be flooded in moonlight. Opening out the folded sheets in her palm, she watched them expand like a living thing.

She pushed the pages under the crack of the shut bathroom door. Elliott backed away.

'I will leave you in peace to read them, but don't take too long,' Janey said curtly.

Walking away from him, she made her way downstairs into the morning room. It had always been her favourite part of the house, the place where the windows gathered the sun best. She sat on the sofa.

Arranging her legs comfortably, she inclined her head to listen to the birds in the overgrown garden.

*

Elliott waited until she had gone. There was an old toilet and a grimy sink in the bathroom. Dad had dropped a couple of towels in there for the boys to use in case they were downstairs. Elliott laid the towels out on the dirty floor tiles so that he had something to sit on. Apart from the diary, he didn't want any part of this old house touching him any more.

He gathered the diary pages together. They still felt warm from Janey's hand.

In a crabbed script Elliott guessed must be Janey's, she'd jotted down the missing lines from the previous cut-off entry. Elliott double-checked the lock on the door was solid. Then, easing himself down, he took an uncertain breath and read the last words ever penned by Theo William Stark.

21

THE LAKE

25th December. Christmas evening. OK. I'm going to record the time because somehow it seems important. It's 8.46 p.m., and it's been dark for hours. I'm trembling as I write this, but sitting here outside the East Wing I'm going to make myself record every detail of the hunt, in case anything happens to me. If it does, this diary had better survive, because I don't want what's happened to my family to happen to anyone else.

*

It all started around quarter past five this afternoon. We'd finished a late Christmas dinner. With everything going on lately, none of us were in the mood to celebrate, and we'd spent most of the meal deciding when we were going to leave Glebe House. Even Mum had had enough now. She and Dad had gone to the back of the house – I can't remember why. I stayed with Eve. No way I was going to leave her alone after the episode with the fence and the stuff in Janey's room.

We were both in the hall. I was looking at one of the portraits. Maybe more than one. I can't remember. I've no idea how long I'd been staring at them. I only remember this: Eve suddenly looked up at me, let out a howling scream and ran from the house.

I went after her. I thought she must have seen Janey behind me or something. I'd been dreading a moment like this – Cullayn using Janey in a last ditch attempt to get to Eve before we left. It was why I was sticking so close to her.

Eve could have fled anywhere, but she took off for the slope, aiming for the hunting ground. I couldn't understand that. I thought Cullayn must be luring her there. It was only afterwards I realised that it was me who drove her in that direction.

It was almost dark already, with snow everywhere. Eve wasn't a fast runner at the best of times, so I had no problem catching her before she got far up the slope. She was wearing her favourite red dress, and for some reason that annoyed me. I grabbed the hem of it and yanked her back. 'Get back indoors!' I shouted, shaking her. 'You idiot! It's not safe out here!'

She dug her nails into me.

'Stop it!' I growled. 'What the hell's the matter with you?'

I wasn't listening to her screams. I wasn't listening to anything. I dragged her across the slope. Terrified, Eve kicked me a couple of times, then reached up to scratch my face. What happened next is a kind of blur. Something inside me exploded with rage. I was so angry I hit Eve. Then – still not understanding what was happening to me – I snatched her left arm and started hauling her up the slope towards the trees.

'You!' Eve screamed.

Her eyes must have been filled with terror, but I wasn't looking. Her endless whimpers only irritated me. Such a stupid kid. 'Shut up!' I yelled. She fought me all the way to the woods. It didn't even occur to me to ask why I was going towards the trees until I heard a rustle from their leaves.

Eve was so scared of me that she managed to yank her hand free. She fell back, whacking her head on a tree root. I heard an awful crack and for a moment she was unconscious, completely still.

'Eve?' I gasped, a tiny part of me still able to respond to her in a normal way. As I leaned over her she woke, opened her eyes. Her mouth was lined with blood. Then, seeing me, she held her hands over her face to protect herself. In that long second, for which I will never forgive myself, she really thought I was going to hit her again, and I realise now that I was about to do just that.

It was not me making the choices.

Somehow Eve squirmed away, stood up and scrambled across the slope. I didn't follow at first. I'd spotted something bright between the trees. There was a clear sky above the wood, and I thought it must be the moon, or a mixture of that and starlight. But then I realised how excited I was, and that it was another kind of light altogether – Cullayn's brightness, orange and red, lighting up the trees.

Moments later the hunter himself appeared. He was standing next to a huge oak, arms folded, rigged out in full hunting leathers. As soon as he had my attention, he wiped his hands on his jacket and headed for Eve. His body crunched across the snow, but at any one moment only his boot or an arm or his swirling beard was visible. I remember shaking my head as for one dizzying second Cullayn and the trees behind him merged, his body wild and at one with each of the trunks.

Eve finally saw him and screamed, stumbling across the slope. But not towards me. Away from us both. I raced across the mud, tracking west.

I know now that I was cutting off Eve's retreat. It never occurred to me to head towards Cullayn, to try to stop him. I was helping him shepherd Eve towards the denser trees on the eastern slope.

Cullayn had no weapons in his hands. I know that because he stopped to show me. He shook out his hunter's cuffs like a magician, proving that he had nothing extra hidden. Then he gave me a triumphant smile, his face shining. It was obvious how happy he was to be on his hunting ground again. *It's OK, he hasn't chosen his weapon for Eve yet*, I remember thinking. I couldn't have been more wrong about that, of course.

At some point I stared down at my hands. Flexed them. *Bared them*. Felt suddenly exhilarated. I was confused by that, but my legs were not confused. They went after Eve.

I caught her. Pulled her down. Before she could scream again, I rammed her mouth against my chest. Turning her face, I held it in a headlock. I'd never used a headlock like that before in my life, but it felt natural. I also remember thinking that it was so disappointingly easy. And I've no doubt what I was going to do next. Only the distraction of the ghost children delayed me.

All four of them were fast-floating down the slope.

I could see them clearly. That fact alone should have warned me that I wasn't myself, but it didn't. I also didn't understand why the ghosts were taking such a risk when Cullayn was so close until I realised that they were heading for *me*. I still had Eve's face twisted in a headlock. I heard her muffled cries, but they only irritated me.

Sam Cosgrove reached me first. Tracing a circle with his fingers around my neck, he *pulled*. Without him actually touching me, it felt like I was inside a choking noose. I fell, groaning, but I still had Eve tight against my chest. Alice flew at me next, but I avoided her, tightening my grip on Eve. Even now I didn't have any doubts about what I was doing.

From the border of the trees Cullayn cheered, willing me on. He'd caught little Leo, and was effortlessly holding him in one arm while beckoning at Nell, encouraging her to attempt a rescue. Sam flew from me, heading in flashes of blue motion across the slope towards Leo. Cullayn saw him and waited.

Eve was still squealing in my headlock. Cullayn caught my eye – reminding me what I was supposed to do – and it was only Janey who stopped me from killing Eve. I've no idea how long she'd been sneaking up behind me, but she didn't stop to ask

questions. She punched me, hard, in the face.
I slumped to the ground, still holding Eve. Before
I could get up again Janey knelt astride my chest
and shoved a small mirror at me.

In it I saw my transformed face. Saw what I looked
like. Felt my chin. The fullness of Cullayn's beard
was in my hands when I shaped it. From across the
slope, Cullayn hissed at Janey.

Dropping Eve, I gasped, finally understanding.
I collapsed to my knees, felt Cullayn's hold on me
fading.

'Eve, I'm ... I'm not after you,' I groaned. 'I'm ...
please ...'

Too late. Eve was already hurrying away. I ran
towards her, shouting, telling her I wasn't going to
hurt her, meaning it this time, but Eve just screamed
louder.

'Let *me* go after her,' Janey shouted.

Nodding, still reeling from what I'd nearly done to
Eve, I gazed up at the upper slope.

Cullayn stood there. He was locked in a fight with
Sam Cosgrove. It was incredible what Sam was doing.
Pinching the air around him, creating tiny spaces in
which to move, he burst in flickers of blue around
Cullayn's body, squeezing between gaps his own
fingers made. Cullayn lashed out again and again,
but Sam was too quick for him and, when Cullayn

reached out with both arms, Leo pulled free with a squeal.

As soon as that happened, all the ghost children fled in different directions.

Cullayn looked disappointed. But only slightly. I could tell he liked the way Sam had extended the hunt. New ideas danced in Cullayn's eyes, and before I could react he was off again down the slope, heading for Janey this time.

Janey was so focused on Eve that she didn't see Cullayn coming. At the last second I screamed a warning to her and she fashioned something complex with her hands to hold him back – folding, dispersing space with her fingers. But Cullayn fought through her defence easily, clamped Janey in a bear-hug and with a cry of absolute triumph vaulted with her all the way to the trees.

In that moment, lit by Cullayn's light, the trunks belonged to him, and they held both Cullayn and Janey aloft, their branches and leaves seething at her throat.

I sprinted towards Janey, but only a ghost could ride the winds fast enough to get there in time, and again Sam never hesitated. He was like a tornado tearing into the heart of the trees. He spread his body, somehow *wrapping* himself around Cullayn's forearm.

Grunting in surprise, Cullayn dropped Janey. Falling from the trees, she took her chance, rubbing her neck as she sprinted away.

Cullayn only seemed to enjoy the setback. He idly swiped a rough hand towards Sam's head, but his gaze was already shifting back in a leisurely way to Eve. She was half way down the slope now, and Cullayn set off after her with a roar. His whole body was bent into the slope, like a lion in a sprint for the kill. Stretching his legs impossibly wide, a single bend of his knee took him one-third of the way down the slope, and suddenly his hands were active as well, juggling weapons. I had been Cullayn's preferred choice for killing Eve, but knives would do, and as he ran Cullayn sharpened three blades across each other, tossed one up, caught it and *threw*.

I don't think Cullayn's aim was intended to kill Eve. He wasn't after anything so simple or quick as that. But it was definitely meant to hurt her. Alice, standing between Cullayn and Eve, made a quick sideways cut with her hand, deflecting it.

Was Cullayn disappointed? No. I could see how little fear he had of Alice's resistance. Conjuring other weapons as he ran after Eve, he was happy, gloating, his hunter's feet striding at his own pace.

I staggered across to Janey. She was clutching her throat. She couldn't breathe properly. 'I'm OK,' she rasped. 'But you have to stop him.'

'How?' I said.

'I don't know. But Eve's just a little girl. Cullayn's not as interested in her as you think. Make *yourself* his target.'

I headed down the snow of the slope. 'Cullayn! Cullayn!' I yelled as loudly as I could.

He glanced back, but he was too caught up in his hunt of Eve to bother with me yet.

Eve was nearly off the slope now, on flat ground. She hadn't stopped screaming for a second, and with huge relief I saw that she must finally have got close enough for Mum and Dad to hear because they both came running out of the house at the same time.

As Mum ran towards Eve, Dad stopped dead in his tracks. He'd spotted Cullayn. And the reason was obvious. Cullayn wasn't disguising himself any more. He *wanted* to be seen. No more hiding. This hunt of adults was far better than any sport Eve could offer, and he hovered next to Mum and Dad in his full form at last, grinning, letting them both get a good long look at him.

Mum swept Eve up into her arms. Seeing that, a burst of orange light flew off Cullayn's tongue, and he soared over the two of them, his arms making chopping, slashing motions.

Mum fell down in a hard shudder, but somehow kept hold of Eve. Picking herself up from the ground, she stood there, fuzzily shaking her head, trying to understand what had happened.

Cullayn wielded his knives, throwing them into the air and catching them impossibly fast, pricking their steel tips alternately against the skin of Mum and Dad's neck, enjoying their reaction.

Mum drew back. She placed Eve behind her so that she was safe. Then she stared at Cullayn with a ferocity I'd never seen from anyone before. And Cullayn *loved* that moment. He loved it. A mother protecting her child. What higher stakes, what better hunt, than this?

I was still sliding as fast as I could down the slope when with a huge snarl Dad crashed into Cullayn's back. Cullayn's weapons spilled on the ground. He seemed winded. But after seeing him fight all this time I knew he wasn't. Huffing like an old man, wriggling comically, apparently unable to free himself from Dad's hold, he reached with a deliberate clumsiness into his belt for a short stabbing sword.

Mum snatched it from him. Looked at it.
I remember that: the direct way she looked at it. She didn't tremble. Didn't need to hear Dad yelling, 'Use

the thing! Use it!' Without hesitation she took the sword in both hands and, with Cullayn abruptly raising his chest, offering himself to her, she plunged the point straight past his ribs into his heart.

Except, no. It wasn't *his* heart she punctured. As the sword came down, Cullayn evaporated in a mist of orange-red, but Mum could no longer hold back. The blade struck, the force of the blow carrying the sword down hard to where now only Dad was. Mum wanted so much to kill Cullayn in that moment, and the blade went straight into the left side of Dad's chest and buried itself to the hilt.

A cry of pure delight shot from Cullayn's lips that lit up the air like a firework display. Standing back at the tree-line he watched Mum, in awe at what he'd achieved. Dad, on the other hand, gazed down at the sword in an almost puzzled way, as if he couldn't quite understand how it had got there.

While Mum bent over Dad in horror, Eve ran. It was not from Cullayn she was running, but me. I'd arrived, but got too close. She still thought I was going to hurt her.

'It's OK!' I shouted. 'I won't do anything to you! Eve!'

'Go after her, Theo!' Mum gasped, holding onto Dad. 'Go on!'

Eve was heading towards the house, and I went to cut her off, but that was a mistake. She saw me and ran in the opposite direction – towards the lake.

There was no sign of Cullayn. Janey was high up the slope, holding her neck in pain. Mum had taken the sword out of Dad's chest and was pressing her hands over the wound, trying to keep him alive.

Eve reached the lake. Without even thinking about what she was doing, she ran straight onto the ice.

No, I thought. Dad had spelled out to us how freezing cold the water is under the ice crust. In temperatures like this you've got a few minutes to get out at most, or you're dead. Eve wasn't thinking about that. She skidded on her flat shoes. Only her lightness prevented the ice from shattering.

I frantically called her name. If she had trusted me in that moment I'd have been able to get her back to shore easily. 'Eve, it's OK,' I said. 'Please listen. I won't hurt you. Just get off the ice!'

She looked at me heart-brokenly. I could tell she wanted to believe me. I could see how scared she was of the ice breaking, and I realise now that she'd have taken anyone's help in that moment except mine. 'Eve!' I called out. 'Come here!' From the shore I held out my hand to reassure her.

Then both of us heard a noise near the house.

It was Mum, crying. I knew it meant that Dad was

dead. Janey reached Mum seconds later, and knelt beside her. Mum didn't seem to notice Janey was there. She clutched Dad to her, sobbing. But a moment later she glanced up, spotted Eve, left Dad with Janey and rushed towards the lake, waving her arms.

It was exactly what Eve needed. She trusted Mum, and she flung her own arms out wide, skidding towards her across the lake. I made sure I stayed well back. But as she got near the shore, Eve slowed down. I didn't understand the reason until I saw the thin crack branching outwards along the ice from the front of her toes.

'*Eve, don't move,*' a voice said. Not mine. Not Mum's. It sounded a bit like Mum's voice. But it was Cullayn, somewhere out of sight, whispering.

And Eve did stay still. Just for a second. But that second was the only one she had left to get to shore before the ice splintered under her. I remember watching Eve gaze down at her own small feet. And then she screamed and lunged for the shore. For a moment I thought she might make it. But the ice sheet shattered, and she fell like a stone into the water.

She bobbed up again seconds later, gasping with the cold, screaming 'Mummy! Mummy!' Terrified, hemmed in by ice, she splashed in a doggy-paddle style out into the middle of the lake instead of back to shore. From her gasps, I could tell how bitterly cold the water was.

It didn't matter how terrified Eve was of me now, I had to get to her. Taking my shoes off to reduce the weight, I stepped onto the ice. It cracked straight away. Swaying, backing off, I tried to think what to do.

'Theo, go to the house!' Mum yelled, running towards me. 'Find something with a long handle!'

I sprinted back to the house. Found a broom in the kitchen.

By the time I got back to the lake there was no sign of Mum or Eve. Where were they?

Then Mum surfaced between sheets of ice. 'I can't find her!' she rasped, already half-frozen. 'I can't—'

Eve suddenly appeared in the water nearby, her uptilted face coughing and spluttering. Mum immediately grasped her with her left arm, holding Eve's face out of the water, and with her right began beating her way back to shore.

They should have made it. Mum was already exhausted from the extreme cold, but she was a good swimmer and I'm sure she was still strong enough to make the bank. If she'd been on her own I think she'd have done it easily. But she was also trying to save Eve, and Eve was panicking.

She kept flailing her arms, hitting Mum, and so Mum had a choice. Either to leave Eve, or take all her weight, battle her panic and try to get them both out.

'Mum, grab the broom!' I yelled. She reached for it, but she had only one hand free, the broom was soon wet and the one time Mum managed to catch it the handle slipped from her grasp.

I kept edging nearer Mum with the broom, but the ice was splitting all around me and Mum was still too far out. She shouted for me to keep back.

I don't know how Mum managed the next thing. It must have been with the last of her strength that she lifted Eve to the surface of the water and flung her towards a wide patch of ice near me.

Eve clung to the ice but still wouldn't grab the broom handle until Janey arrived and held it out to her. From there she reached Janey's outstretched arms. Soaking wet, shivering, Eve made small crying noises, but she was safe.

That fact brought a brief smile of wonder to Mum's frozen face. I kept telling her to swim, but her arms were too numb.

'Keep going!' I pleaded, seeing that she was barely moving now.

'I can't any more,' she told me simply. 'I can't. I'm done.'

And as she said that she gazed steadily at me, and at Eve, and it was as if she was drinking us in, trying to remember us in some way for whatever was to come. And then I saw a look on Mum's face that I'll never forget.

'Oh God, Theo,' she whispered. 'I'm so sorry to leave you like this. We love you both. Always ... always know that. Look after your sister.' Then, gently, as if a wave had simply washed over her head, she dropped beneath the surface of the water and was gone.

*

That's it. That's all of it. Three hours later I'm sitting here, inside the house. I can't believe I'm safe while Mum and Dad are dead. THEY ARE DEAD. The only reason I'm alive is that Janey somehow held onto me, preventing me from jumping in after Mum. I've got a vague memory after that of Janey rubbing the shivering Eve, wrapping her up in her own dress, warming her body up.

But Eve wanted Dad. She pulled away from Janey and ran towards him. She lifted his neck up, trying to make him listen. She didn't realise he was dead. Then, finally understanding, she just ran and ran towards the main doors of the house. That's when

Cullayn reappeared. Gliding like a skimming stone across the lake's surface, he settled unseen behind Eve and followed her inside.

I set off after them, but had to stop for Janey. She'd started choking. Her neck was in a terrible state where Cullayn had squeezed it. She could barely breathe by the time I got her home, it was so swollen. Her parents answered the door, and for once they did something good for her, getting into their car and taking Janey to hospital.

Since then I've been looking for Eve. I know she's hiding somewhere inside the house, scared of Cullayn but also scared of me. I don't want her to be scared of me. I can't believe I let Cullayn get to me like that. I can't believe the way I hit Eve and held her in that headlock. If I find her, I'll just guide her gently. I won't go near her. I'll just lead her to the village, where other people can help us. I'm going to stop writing now and look again for Eve. I have to find her.

*

It's 9.35 p.m. I just called the police. I explained what had happened to Mum and Dad. I can tell the woman on the phone didn't believe me, especially when I told her about Cullayn, but they're sending someone.

9.42. A moment ago, I heard Eve's voice. It was very distant but I'm sure it was coming from the East Wing. Maybe Cullayn dragged her in there. Or maybe Eve ran in there to hide from me. I don't know. But I'm going in there to have a look. Wish me luck.
I don't even know why I'm recording this. I don't know who might read it. If you are a stranger, I just hope you're not stuck in this terrible house. Whoever you are, I hope that you're somewhere safe, a long way from here. I wish I could see your face. How old are you? I wish I knew what you look like. Whoever is reading this diary, I really wish you were with me right now. I wish someone was.

Theo Stark

22
DON'T YOU TRUST ME?

Elliott stopped reading. The diary ended there. A signature was the last thing Theo ever wrote. The ink of his name stood out on the page like a final bold statement.

Numbly, Elliott clenched the last diary page in both hands, staring at the paper as if by sheer willpower he could reveal the fate of Theo and Eve. Why hadn't Theo come back to record what happened next?

Elliott had so much admiration for Theo in that moment. He couldn't imagine the strength it must have taken for him to go into the East Wing, knowing Cullayn was there – to go after Eve simply because it was the right thing to do.

My friend, Elliott thought, his mouth compressed with emotion. With all of his heart he wished he could go back fifty years in time. Either to stop Theo going inside the East Wing, or to be there at his side. Theo was dead. Elliott was absolutely sure of it, and he felt closer in that moment to Theo than he had to anyone else in his life except Ben and Dad. And thinking about *them* brought him back to the present.

Standing up, Elliott unlocked the bathroom to confront Jane Amanda Roberts.

She was outside the door. She had made her way up from the sunshine heat of the morning room. Wary and thin, tense and still, she observed him closely. Despite the last diary entry, Elliott still had no idea whether or not he could trust her.

'So,' she said briskly, 'you have the facts now. Cullayn didn't hang around to offer evidence to the police. The only verdict that made sense to them was that of a wife who inexplicably went insane, stabbed her husband and killed her own children. It looked like she'd drowned herself afterwards in the lake. I offered the police the true story, but you can imagine what they made of that. They drained the lake, expecting to find Eve and Theo's bodies. Didn't. Commenced an exhaustive search of the house. Still couldn't find them. Embarrassing for the police. Not being able to find the bodies, I mean. But clearly the mother had disposed of them somewhere. A loose end, but the officers on the case lived with it.'

Elliott gave her a belligerent stare. 'Why didn't the police find the bodies?'

'Because Cullayn hid them first, of course.'

'Where?'

'His secret room inside the East Wing. It's all in the

diary. A compartment. Beautifully concealed. It's where his heart is, you might say.' She gave Elliott an astute look. 'Don't pretend you don't know what I'm talking about.'

Elliott thought of the smooth wall inside the dark passageway.

'Yes,' Janey said, reading his expression. 'The descending floor. The steps. Such a little staircase, but so hard to walk down, eh? The police searched the East Wing for days, but they weren't looking for a concealed room. Poor Eve and Theo were lying entombed in graceless silence long before the investigation was complete.'

'How do you know that?' Elliott demanded, keeping his distance.

Janey looked impatient. 'Because Eve told me. I met her weeks later. She was dead, of course, but not yet the tainted thing she is now. Cullayn hadn't quite got his full clutches into her then.' Janey picked at her fingernails. 'You want to know what happened to Theo?'

Elliott glared at Janey, wanting to shut her up, but needing the truth.

'I don't trust you,' he said. 'You're working with Cullayn. In the diary Theo says Cullayn possessed you.'

'That was briefly,' Janey snapped. 'I shook his influence off for good afterwards.'

'Don't give me that!' Elliott shouted. 'You opened

up the East Wing! You think I didn't see the screwdriver?'

'I had no choice about that,' Janey said. 'I had to pretend I was co-operating with Cullayn.'

'Why?'

'I can't reveal that yet. You're going to have to trust me.'

Elliott stared fiercely at her. Did he trust her? No. But if he was going to have any chance of rescuing Dad and Ben, he knew he needed an ally. Janey was the only one available. Her dress was still adorned with the favourite flowers of the ghost children. That reminder of the old ghost-caring Janey made Elliott decide to keep an open mind.

'You know from the diary that Theo responded to Eve's shouts for help,' Janey said. 'I suspect that Eve was already ensconced in Cullayn's secret room by then. Everything he did was leading her there. The room's a trap, of course. The handle to open the door from inside ceased working in Cullayn's time, even if Eve could have reached it. A nice irony that. Killing her the same way *he* was killed. That would definitely have appealed to Cullayn. No way out of the room, except via his powers, and he wanted her dead. Looking for Eve, Theo eventually made his way inside the secret room as well.' Janey hesitated. 'If it makes you feel any better, Eve told me that Theo cradled her head at the very end. Her last living memory was of him telling her stories of hope, and holding her.'

Elliott tried to take that in. 'So Theo was still alive when Eve died. He outlasted her.'

'Yes. He died a day or so later. I sensed it. So did the ghost-children. I assume he departed the same way as his parents, went peacefully onward. It's so hard for the ghosts to stay rooted to our world.'

Elliott shook his head. 'No. Theo would never have left Eve alone. Never.'

Janey threw her head back and laughed. It was a bitter noise.

'You give insufficient credit to the owner of Glebe House, Elliott. Theo had to depart, and quickly, or Cullayn would have snatched his spirit as surely as his sister's. However, you're right. There must have been some kind of battle at the moment of death. Theo was a special boy. Cullayn must have been waiting eagerly on his last breath to gather his spirit for himself. Somehow Theo eluded him. I'd like to have witnessed that. I might have learned something about shortcutting this long journey had I seen how Theo accomplished it. Even so, patience, your unwitting help and that of your brother and your father have brought us to where we are now.' She offered Elliott a small bow.

He gave her a hard look.

'I see you still trust me even less than you like me,'

she said. 'I always knew I'd have to do this alone. But trust me or not, do you believe that Cullayn has Ben and your father?'

Elliott reluctantly nodded.

'Then you are not a complete fool after all, and maybe that offers us an advantage.'

'What advantage?'

'Two of us to divide Cullayn's attention.'

Elliott assessed the sarcastic, scheming woman in front of him. Was this really the girl Theo had admired so much? Yet, thinking about it, hadn't Janey possessed the very same traits in those days, only as part of a more rounded personality? Perhaps the only way she'd survived the bitterness of these past fifty years was to dig deep into scorn.

'You've changed,' he said.

'Yes,' Janey admitted, her look only briefly sad. 'She's irrecoverable, that silly, naive version of me. I stopped thinking of her about forty years ago. Anyhow, we can chat away if you wish, but, remember, every minute we stand debating here your father is that same minute closer to death. He's lost a lot of blood already.'

Elliott tensed, studying Janey. 'What are you planning to do in there?' he asked uneasily.

'Stalk the hunter, claim his power, make him grovel for forgiveness and offer none, that sort of thing.' Janey gave Elliott a disarmingly intense smile. 'Cullayn wants only one thing.'

'To hunt.'

'Exactly. The everlasting hunt. The power to leave Glebe House and roam the world. And Ben's going to help the owner achieve his goal. We haven't got long before Cullayn shoves him onto the hunting ground.'

'What about Dad?'

'Amusement value only, but to Cullayn that means a lot. Come on,' Janey said tetchily. 'We can't wait here. We need to reach in by the backdoor while Cullayn's still cooing over his new acquisitions.'

'The backdoor?'

'I haven't got time to explain everything, Elliott.' Without waiting for further questions, Janey turned around and began walking at a fair clip down the staircase. Elliott hesitated, then raced after her, catching up once she was outside the East Wing.

'Look inside the darkness,' Janey said curtly. 'Face it.'

Elliott hesitated. Inside the entrance a few chinks of daylight suffused the otherwise murky entrance corridor.

'Afraid?' she challenged him.

'Yes,' he admitted.

'Good. Fear gives you an edge, but too much leaves you cringing and useless. I allowed you two journeys inside to get over that.'

'What about you?' Elliott challenged her back. 'Your

tricks didn't work last time against Cullayn, did they?'

'I know others now.'

Elliott flinched as without warning Janey thrust her hand into the air of the East Wing's open entrance. A dizzying sensation followed, the air seeming to stretch as if the focus of the universe had momentarily flexed. Then Janey curled one of her arthritic hands, and with the singular intent of a bird of prey dragged her open fingers brutally backward.

Her blue eyes narrowed as something *caught*.

Then she yanked hard, seeking a fuller hold with two more fingers.

'The entrance is already open,' Elliott pointed out.

'My way inside, not his.'

Janey tugged harder, gripping the air, determined. Moments later Elliott felt rather than heard something *detach*, and next he knew Janey had hold of his hand, and her entire outline was flaring with apricot-hued light as strand by strand she hauled her once-dark hair through the divide, and Elliott with it. Elliott screamed, every cord in his neck taut with pressure as Janey heaved her old body and his younger one into the East Wing.

'Hurry,' she ordered, when he resisted her tug. 'I can't keep this open forever! It's only a trick to enter without him seeing. A reshaping of air. Come on!'

Elliott wavered – then let her drag him inside.

He fell forward onto the burgundy carpet. Close up,

it smelled of mould and dry rot. He stood up fast, prepared to defend himself. The entrance corridor was the same dark length it had always been.

'Too gloomy for you?' Janey inquired. 'I agree. Cullayn's had his way for far too long. Let's change things.' She raised the index finger of her right hand and suddenly the entire corridor was bathed in bluish light. 'That's better,' she said. 'A parlour trick only, but useful. You can let go of my hand now, by the way.'

Elliott did so.

Pasted to the wall on their left was a portrait. It showed Janey being chased into the hunting ground by Cullayn. It was not an oil painting but a new sketch, quick and crude.

'I see Cullayn's asked Eve to pen me a greeting card,' Janey said tartly. 'How nice. It means he knows I'm coming but, since he's not here to greet me himself, not quite when.'

She smiled. Elliott couldn't believe she could react with such calm equanimity to the picture, and, though he still didn't trust her, it did give him more confidence. She casually knocked the sketch to the floor and kicked it away. 'Oops.'

The next sketch on the same wall stopped Elliott dead. It was one of *him* being chased up the slope – chased by a triumvirate: Eve, Cullayn and Ben.

'Just another little gift to scare us,' Janey said evenly.

'Don't look at the pictures or do, Elliott, whatever.' She shrugged dismissively. 'Cullayn likes to gather you in with his artwork. He always overestimated his talent in that regard in my view, and Eve's hardly improved under his tutelage.'

'Is that where his power is?' Elliott asked, amazed at her flippancy. 'In the portraits?'

'Partly.' Janey allowed herself a tinkle of dark laughter. 'It's only paint, though. Always was. Daubs. Smudges. But invested with the owner's will, sufficient to guide an unwitting eye. Enough, if you look for long enough, to show you what he wants. To snare Ben.'

'And you,' Elliott noted, thinking of the diary.

'Indeed. My eyes were ever drawn to his goofy teeth.'

Janey punched a hole directly through the sketch of Elliott, inviting him to do the same. He did.

'Feel better?'

Elliott nodded.

'Good.' Janey began moving smoothly down the now well-lit corridor. She never slackened her pace or speeded up or altered her path by even one degree, confident in where her stride was taking her. From time to time she casually ripped portraits from their mounts and dumped them on the carpet.

'Why do you keep doing that?' Elliott asked.

'Because he won't like it. So we should keep doing it, eh? Stop skulking behind me, Elliott. That's what

Cullayn likes, bringing everyone to their knees.'

'But if we mess with the portraits won't he know we're here?'

'The portraits don't report to him, Elliott,' Janey said, amused. 'Those in the house are positioned to ensnare his victims. Inside here, they merely serve to terrorise. We'll be long gone before he finds out what we've done to his precious little babies.'

Janey sped up. The shadows of the East Wing retreated at the rise of her finger. In no time at all they passed three intersection points.

'Ben ran a little too fast into this,' Janey muttered, patting a wall. 'I apologise for that. An accident. Only a bump on the head, however. Better than Cullayn getting hold of him.'

'Why didn't Cullayn just grab Ben the first time he came in?'

'And end the fun just like that?' Janey snapped her fingers. 'Surely you've learned by now that Cullayn likes to extend his pleasure. Especially since he's had such lean pickings recently. Poor man. No fresh guts to spill on his hunting ground. Plus there's the small matter that this time he wanted to blood Eve on the hunt. She's his little protégée. He wants her in on the act. He's been preparing her for this moment for a very long time. Is she ready to kill in cold blood? Even Cullayn's not sure. We'd better hope she is not.'

Janey's dark eyes twinkled. Elliott had no idea what to make of her carefree sarcasm. It was the perfect antidote to the brooding atmosphere of the East Wing, but was it real or only to dispel her own fear?

'Fifty years ago you tried to stop Cullayn and failed,' he said. 'You were confident that time as well.'

'I had a lot of sincerely earnest passion then, didn't I?' she admitted. 'Spent hours and hours chatting away to ghost kids, winsomely dallying around graves. That idiot girl's gone. I had my gift, but not one clue what to do with it.'

'Do you now?'

'Oh yes. Keep up, Elliott,' she said amiably, 'and watch out for an attack from the side corridors. We're getting close to the heart of the East Wing. I doubt Cullayn will let us get there without a surprise or two.'

'He's listening, isn't he?' Elliott said. 'He's listening right now.'

Janey appraised Elliott a moment. 'Indeed. Cullayn's ever a curious, scenting presence, especially here in his filthy digs. A mind tuning in, as it were. He will not know exactly where we are, but he'll be catching snatches of our conversation. So we must be careful what we offer him, mustn't we?' She gave Elliott a quiet, measured look. 'If he senses any weakness, he'll not hesitate to exploit it. Remember the way he had you screaming like a little boy in here? He loves that sound. He'd like to hear it again.'

A chill crept through Elliott. 'You saw that? You were here when it happened? You let him do that to me?'

Janey folded her arms. 'Surely you realise I did more than that? I had to help him scare you as much as I could. Cullayn was watching, wouldn't have accepted anything less. Anyway, whatever use you are here now is only because I let him panic you then.'

When she saw Elliott staring furiously at her, Janey shook her head.

'You used us as bait,' Elliott said, outraged.

'Of course,' she grunted. 'How else to encourage the hunter back to the field of play? The diary was useful. A joy, actually. Bless Theo for writing it. So handy. All those emotions close to the heart. I only had to divide it into tasty morsels and open the East Wing so that Ben went in. I knew he'd be curious. Cullayn's portraits had already led him in there, but the diary was just a little extra push to keep him thinking about it. Eve found Ben first, actually, fey flit little thing that she is. But I knew she'd skip off to tell Daddy all about him.'

Janey's tone left Elliott wanting to hit her.

'I had to,' she said. 'Cullayn knows I'm still the only one who can stop him, so he planned to stay in this house until I was dead and gone to the other side. He'd never have come out in the open without an incentive.

I had to provide him with that, get him to trust me, get in his good books. This was the only way to do it. If Cullayn escapes from Glebe House, he'll go on killing forever.'

'How do you stop him?'

'*Ghost ways.*' When Elliott frowned, Janey flattened her palms together. 'Look. See? No gap between my fingers, yes? And yet ...' She gradually opened her fingers again, creating a three-dimensional pocket between her hands ' ... space where it was not. From nothing, something. The question is how to use it.'

Elliott stared dubiously at her.

'The ghosts travel in the breaches of our world, Elliott,' Janey told him, looking tired. 'Interruptions between surfaces, openings, wherever those may be. Walls are not solid. Bricks have pores. Skilled ghosts, like Cullayn, like dear Sam, make their *own* breaches and use them. Sam's had a whole lifetime with me to perfect my understanding.' Janey steepled her fingers and brought her thumbs together below, creating a lozenge-shaped opening. 'Try to get though the gap,' she said. Elliott prodded his finger at it. Felt resistance in the invisible air where there should have been none. Pressed harder. Found his finger slipping sideways, deflected.

Janey smiled and reached for a door handle leading off the hall. 'Let's try this room, shall we?'

'Wait,' Elliott said. 'Answer this first. You admit you used my family to get to Cullayn. But how were you going to stop him before he did something really bad to us?'

When Janey answered it was the first time he saw a chink in her confidence.

'I had ways,' she muttered.

'No, you didn't, did you?' Elliott said, reading her expression accurately. 'You didn't expect it to be anything like this bad. Cullayn's more powerful than you realised. You've overestimated yourself again. Look at Eve—'

'Pffft, Eve.' Janey waved her fingers. 'A child. And it still took Cullayn half a century to turn her into what she is now. See how weak he is, Theo? On the evening of your arrival, Ben's distant snoring was already of more interest to her than anything Cullayn could offer. She's still a child at heart. Remember that. We're depending on it.'

Janey gave Elliott a fierce warning glare – *shut up, say nothing more* – and then said loudly, 'Such righteous anger in the boy, Cullayn. Do you hear his whine? Are you listening? The pair of us have made quite an adverse impression on him. He doesn't understand yet that the only reason he is still alive is because you are enjoying the game. He thinks it's all about right and wrong. He doesn't seem to grasp that the only important question is whether he is just going to sit down and cry when you

211

start to chase him, or instead do whatever he must to keep his father and brother alive.' She glared at Elliott. 'Well, are you?'

'*Are you?*' Elliott shouted back.

'I'm here for other reasons,' Janey tutted brusquely. Then she yawned, looking sideways at him. 'But honestly, Elliott, why on earth have I bothered to get you to join me in here? You'll give in at the first hurdle, I can tell. You're hardly even worth the price of admission. Are you really ready to risk everything for your father and Ben?'

Elliott hesitated, but only for a second.

'Yes,' he said.

Janey gave him an elaborate curtsey, executed with genuine grace.

'*In that case, challenge is made and set,*' she stated, raising her chin. Her voice was abruptly bell-loud and clear, the announcing of a summons. Then she stepped away from Elliott – as if offering room for someone else to enter the space between them.

'It's a fair fight, guv'nor,' Janey said to Elliott, falling into slang. She laughed. 'You came willingly enough, boy. I didn't lead you in or promise a damn thing. Cullayn always prefers his guests to be willing. So, we'll do it. We will *have it.*' She looked to the corridor end and in a clipped tone cried, 'Let the hunter and the hunted converge!'

Elliott felt his stomach clench. 'You *are* working with Cullayn!' he rasped.

He waited, open-mouthed. He knew something terrible was about to happen, and then it did happen.

He heard a sound: the opening of a door, the opening of many doors.

Janey sniffed, leaning casually against the nearest wall. She picked idly at her nails. 'Cullayn's right about one thing,' she said. 'The longer I'm in this place the more I realise it's not at its best in these floodlights. Too garish. Shadows and dark work better with this particular decor.'

She flicked a petal off her dress. 'You think you know darkness, Elliott,' she said. 'But it comes in many forms. There is darkness, and then again there is darkness akin to the final darkness that will arrive for us all at the end of the world. That's what I'm going to give you now. That's *Cullayn's darkness*.' As she raised her hands, a shiver of terror passed though Elliott.

'No!' he yelled, but Janey laughed and brought her hands together, and as she did so every mote of light in the East Wing was snuffed out.

23

TAKE MY HAND

The darkness was absolute, supreme, pure, utter.

'Quick!' Janey hissed, dragging Elliott towards her. 'Now's our chance. Even Cullayn needs some light to find us. And I've extinguished every bit. We must get away from here!'

'No, you're working for *him*!' Elliott thundered. 'Get away.' He shoved at her in the total darkness. 'I won't do anything you say.'

'Don't be a fool,' she growled in his ear. 'That was just a show! He was listening! Haven't you learned anything yet? Don't give him any advantage. Only surefootedness will save us.' She created a tiny candle brightness in her hand and held it out in front of her, already striding away. 'This light and no more. Can you see me? Wait.' She stopped, with a flick of her hands cupped her ears. 'There. He can't hear us. Not until he gets close.'

Elliott stayed where he was.

'Take my hand,' Janey insisted. When he did not she strode impatiently towards him. 'You're right, Elliott,' she whispered. 'I *did* underestimate him, but he was eavesdropping on our conversation and I couldn't have him knowing my mistake. I delivered him everything – Ben and your father all packaged up, and he thinks I'm delivering you, too. He thinks I'm still in his pocket, or he would not have even allowed me in here. Don't you understand? Everything I did was to get us *this far inside*. From here we can go to where we have to be. The knight's room. It's our only chance.'

When Elliott still did not trust her, Janey's voice became urgent. 'Not directly, but by the backdoor, Elliott. I told you! Via the link. Via Eve. The two of them together are way too powerful for me to face. We've got to get her alone. This is the only way.'

Elliott reluctantly followed Janey down the corridor as she hurried, illuminated by the hand's width band of light. 'I'm sorry I had to put you through that performance,' she said, 'but Cullayn gave me a plan to follow and I had to go part-way with him. Eve's the key. She's been here so long that almost half of Cullayn's power has dribbled into her. That's why you can see her. She's made of the same powerful stuff as Cullayn now. And that's our advantage. Because if we can snatch her out, separate them, I might be strong enough to fight him on my own.'

'How do we separate them?' Elliott demanded, trembling but determined Janey wouldn't see it.

'We coax her. That's the plan. What's the one thing in the East Wing that makes you stop and gaze, Elliott?'

'The portraits.'

'And for Eve, one portrait in particular. I'm not sure why she's so fixated on it, but even Cullayn's attention wavers sometimes, and when it does there's one room, and a single figure, that she always hurries off to see. Cullayn will already be sniffing us out. But he won't come himself, not at first. He'll send Eve. She'll probably hide from us, but I know which room she'll enter. She won't be able to resist it. And we'll briefly have her to ourselves.'

Janey kept the pace up, but from her occasional stumbles Elliott could tell she was beginning to tire. She guided him right and left, and left again, until they were in a corridor that to him looked identical to all the others. There she stopped, flexing her fingers with a flourish. As her fingertips parted, the dim natural daylight of the East Wing returned.

'We need to invite her in,' Janey explained.

They entered the second room on the right of the corridor. Inside, there was a window. It was the first window Elliott had seen in the East Wing and, predictably, it looked towards the slope of the hunting ground.

'This room is the place Cullayn always brought his

victims just before the hunt,' Janey said. 'He liked them to get a good eyeful of what was in store.'

She closed the door behind them and Elliott studied the room. Apart from the window it seemed as elaborately anonymous as all the other bedrooms he'd seen in the East Wing.

'You'd better tell me what you're going to do in here, or I'm not helping you,' he said. 'I mean it. Tell me now.'

Janey opened her hand, allowing light to spill between her fingers. 'Keep your voice down,' she warned. 'Do you see what makes this room so different?'

'No.'

'No?'

'There's just the usual furniture, and . . . oh.'

Elliott saw it now. There were no portraits of Cullayn. Instead, behind him, a huge picture hung over the bed. The picture was not a painting but an intricately-embroidered tapestry. It depicted an ancient medieval battleground, and at the calm centre of that battleground was a knight. He sat on a white horse, holding a gleaming sword aloft in defiance of whole armies scattered like insects across the tapestry. It was a spell-binding scene. The knight was life-sized, and armed with mace and lance as well as sword. There was something magnificent about the way he was rearing up on his horse against seemingly impossible odds. Seeing the knight's heroic stance in the crippled setting of the East Wing for some reason made Elliott stand up straighter.

Janey glanced from the tapestry back to Elliott. 'Artwork can have a power beyond the value Cullayn puts upon it, eh? I suspect he tolerates its presence because he fancies himself as the knight. He doesn't realise he's one of the maggot-soldiers on the plains below. But the reason *we* care about the picture is that Eve comes here. She stares at this picture all the time. I've followed her, seen her reaction. It makes her heart swirl with emotion.'

'Why?'

'Can't you guess?'

Elliott studied the tapestry closely. 'Because Cullayn's not in it?'

'Yes. Partly. This is the only room where he is not present. I have checked them all to be sure. But also ...' Janey leaned forward. 'Eve *wants* a knight to come and rescue her, Elliott,' she whispered with sudden passion. 'I'm sure of it. If only she knew it, she wants to be rid of Cullayn. She's desperately lonely in the way only a child can be. The whole house is saturated with her loneliness. Surely you've felt that? But she's got no way out. Cullayn's kept her close, never offered her that choice. I think that if we give her half a chance Eve will join us.'

Elliott almost laughed. 'We're her knights in shining armour?'

'Yes.'

'But how do we make her come with us?'

'Shush,' Janey said under her breath. 'She's here.'

Janey extinguished the light in her hand and hustled Elliott into a shadowed corner behind the door.

Daylight illuminated the room from the window, falling like a bar across the embroidered knight. Elliott waited nervously, and as he did so Eve entered.

She was singing a quiet rhyme about one of the dead boys, about Leo, but it ended when she took her first step inside. Just as Janey had predicated, Eve stopped in front of the tapestry and quickly knelt down. She smoothed out her red dress and crossed her legs under her. She was silent. If you could say it of anyone in the East Wing, she looked content.

'Eve,' Janey whispered.

Elliott heard the quaver in her voice, the anxiety. It was the first time he realised that Janey was herself deeply afraid, and he turned to Eve to see how she reacted.

Eve gasped, looking back at them with an exaggerated *O*. Then she smiled, grinning in a way that made Elliott realise the initial gasp of surprise had been staged – a bit of fun.

'I thought you'd be here,' she said.

Janey had been moving tentatively towards Eve, but now she stopped. 'Did you?'

'Yes, at least Daddy thought so. He got me to do a drawing for you when you arrived. I took ages over it. Do you want to see it?'

Eve reached into the inside pocket of her dress and pulled out a folded piece of creamy-white paper. In overlapped lines of hard pencil, she had sketched the entire present scene in the room. There was the knight rearing up in the tapestry. There was Eve kneeling on the worn carpet beneath it. There was an old woman peering at the sketch, looking baffled.

Elliott heard a tight, compressed wheeze from Janey. He didn't know what the noise meant at first. Then he sensed it was fear – that he was witnessing the wholesale wreckage of all Janey's plans. Cullayn *had* been waiting for her. She hadn't outwitted him. He'd predicted she'd come here. Dangled Eve as a prize. All Janey's subtle traps, turns and tricks were for nothing.

'Welcome,' Eve said, her tone child-like but abruptly pitched like ice. And she bowed – but not to them.

Elliott did not need to be told whom she was honouring.

Janey registered Cullayn's presence before Elliott, and fervently raised her hands to increase the light in the room, but that gesture was not enough to ward him off.

Eve chuckled, and Elliott became aware of stirrings

around him so centuries-old and deeply wrought that their intent was unfathomable.

The light began to fade.

For a few moments Janey struggled against the dimming, held it in check. Then she dropped her hands, gave a terrible groan of defeat, and the room flared red and orange as the master of Glebe House brought his long-considered plans into place.

The air thrummed and shifted of its own accord.

Janey backed against a wall.

'He's coming!' Elliott shouted at her. 'You have other things you can do, don't you? It's *him*! You brought us in here. You must know what to do next!'

Janey clung to the wall. She looked like she might snap. The light was being unmade in front of her eyes and she did nothing except gape at Elliott in bewilderment, her face shaking in soundless fear.

It was, of course, exactly the reaction Cullayn had been waiting for before he made his grand entrance.

'What time is it?' boomed a voice from the darkness as brash as the midday sun.

'Five minutes to midnight,' Eve answered at once, standing to attention.

'Five to midnight?' the voice questioned. It was full of odd, light tones, far more melodious and lively than Elliott had expected. 'High time, then. High time. No victory ever so sweet as this, Janey, or so longed for.

Once you danced to my door to give battle, but now I see you come in secret with a boy in tow. Was it truly with such obvious artifice as your sleight-of-hand entry and these tricks of light that you intended to unman me? Yet I am an owner with simple appetites. A simple man.'

'A simple man,' Eve echoed.

'Yes. The hunter always,' the voice said from the darkness. 'Therefore shall we continue with this fine game of ours, Janey? So far we have merely tested our intentions and resolve with lights, fingers and wagging tongues. That's a beginning, but shall we now prepare for the hunting ground?' The voice waited, as if expecting an answer from Janey. When none came, it gave a loud guffaw of absolute triumph and suddenly all eyes turned to the centre of the room.

24

PICK A WEAPON!

The air swirled with meticulously-crafted points of light. Like stars erupting from slowly condensing nebulae, the points joined to form an outline. It was the outline of a shoulder and arm – a hunter's arm, gathering itself, balanced to strike.

Eve knew her place. She now stepped smartly aside.

Cullayn's lustrous beard grew before them. He was very proud of his beard. Bathed in a persecution of shimmering light, initially it was only a faint flowing of hair, stubble on the rise. Then its whole girth came loose to sparkle against the room's darkness. First the beard, then the mouth, writhing, a near-purr of contentment on lips that were already open and ready to command. Above the mouth, two stars globed into circles and, as they levelled their radiance on Elliott and Janey with terrible purpose, Cullayn detached himself like a nightmare kissed into life from the darkness.

He was already half the hunter: he was never anything less. Feet trussed and booted, peaked hat angled rakishly with child-like pride, he brushed his close-cropped curls. Cullayn did not waste time. Even now, as Elliott watched in dismay, the hunter was girding his limbs, preparing for the joy of the fight ahead. He brought one of his muscular forearms up to fasten the brass buttons of a sturdy leather long-coat. His other arm tightened a black-buckled belt.

Once he was ready he smiled indulgently, glowing with light, and raised both hands.

'A game!' he bellowed. 'A game, if you will!'

Next moment a variety of weapons appeared above his head. Cullayn juggled them in a conjuror's circle: guns, whips, stones, arrowheads, swords, flames, all kept constantly aloft.

'Pick one, pick a weapon!' Cullayn said, turning his gaze on Elliott. 'At least have guts enough to choose *one* this time!' He laughed, spitting out a sod of cold phlegm large enough to fill a mouth. His rough voice was that of a market street trader. 'Or pick two!' he cried. 'I offer you choices of dispatch! Two for the price of one! What do you say, kind sir?' Cullayn bowed and in a practised and elegant move knelt, whipped off his hat and spread his fare of weapons like a feast before Elliott.

Elliott did not know what to do: not pick, and perhaps Cullayn would cut him down where he stood; pick, and he knew the hunting ground would fast follow.

Cullayn gave Eve a cheery wink and offered the

weapons to her instead. 'So choose for the boy,' he said. 'He's shy.'

'A bit of blood will cure that,' Eve said. 'A bit of his own.'

'It will, it will,' Cullayn replied, immensely pleased by her words. Eve giggled as the knives and swords clattered around her feet.

Elliott backed away across the floor. So far he'd seen Eve as the innocent party in all this, but her ruthless words, that giggle and the way she touched and felt the blades made him doubt there was any innocence left.

Janey said nothing. She did not even glance up. Her head was bent. She suddenly looked remarkably old, her neck thin enough to break with or without Cullayn's intervention.

'I've offered Eve a part in the final moments of your hunt,' Cullayn said to Elliott. He made it sound like good news. 'Not too big a part. She's only a little girl.' He and Eve both laughed when he said that. 'But she's anxious to play her role, aren't you, Evey?'

Eve smiled at him and made a moue with her mouth, snatching the weapons up, pretending to like none of them. She picked a whip, threw it back. Picked a net, discarded it.

'So, the little girl's all a-flutter! She can't decide! She's all agog!' Cullayn beamed, the points of light forming his mouth writhing counter-clockwise to the beard.

He squarely faced Elliott. 'You're not sure I'm real, are you boy? You think I'm just a set of cruel intentions buried inside a light display. Janey never understood what would happen if she let Ben in here. She never grasped that even without the first gusts of his life-force in my gut' – Cullayn hugged his stomach in –'even without Ben's death, I'd be more than she could ever handle.' Cullayn sighed contentedly, smashing a leisurely fist into the ground as if he had so much surplus energy that he had to find an outlet for it. The floor shook. 'But what next?' he said. 'Not long now before your brother's dead, Elliott. It's nothing personal, but I'll have Ben's strength, you understand? And I'll have yours, too. A hunter can never have too much stamina.'

Elliott could tell that Cullayn was waiting for a reaction from him, so he gave none. But he couldn't help sneaking a look at Janey.

'No, she's no ideas left,' Cullayn said, almost regretfully. 'I've seen that look on her face before, haven't I, Janey? No good looking to the old nag for anything, Elliott. You're on your own.' Cullayn brought Eve close and hugged her tight. 'Look at this!' he said to her. 'They came to rescue you from the castle, but they forgot about the ogre in the moat, didn't they?'

'And he was all ready for 'em!' she squealed back.

'He was! He was! He splashed out and grabbed 'em!'

Cullayn looked delighted as he swung back to Elliott.

'Ah, listen,' he said, offering a magnanimous snort. 'There's honesty in you coming so willingly into my home to save your brother and your father. I'll give you a fair chase for that, boy, and dispatch you sharply when it's time to be done. But what does Janey deserve? What's she done to improve herself in all these years? A lifetime of self-loathing and fretting. What's that worth, Elliott? What respect has she earned?'

Cullayn knelt down, tapped Janey's bony knees. 'She's such a coward, such a wretched cowardly woman. She never dared come into my East Wing again till your family arrived, Elliott. Did she tell you that? Too scared, she was. But she wanted so much, poor girl. Still does. To free the ghost-children, of course. But to prove herself as well, to feel the special power of defeating me on such a day as this, to follow through truly, despite the fear, and what's more to do the right thing, even by you.'

Cullayn smiled, his whole lower jaw pressing towards Janey like a hyena. 'And then to gracefully retire and say adieu to all her cares. To finally gain her well-deserved peace. There's a mildewed bench in the graveyard, Elliott. It's virtually as old as her. Our Janey likes that seat. Looks over the south downs, it does, lovely little view, and I've seen the wistful look she has there sometimes. I understand her better than she knows herself. She'd love to know that the ghost children have passed on because they've vanquished the evil owner of Glebe House, and then – ah! – then to be able to sit alone in peace at last, on her stupid bench, curled up with a racy book.'

Cullayn shook with laughter. 'That's quite a set of ambitions, isn't it, Elliott? That's something worth drinking to, eh?' He thumbed towards Janey, who was still backed against the wall, staring mutely into space. 'Here's the thing, though. That's all just rubbish in her head. But what do you think Janey fears most?'

Elliott did not reply. He was too frightened to say anything.

'Tongue need loosening?' Cullayn asked. 'I can help with that. I *will* help with that. But first let's have a little hunt.' He turned back to Eve. 'What do you say, Evey?'

'A hunt for the brave boy!' Eve called out, and Cullayn laughed.

Levelling his glowing eyes on Elliott, Cullayn pretended to hide his next words from Eve behind his big hand. 'Eve likes to hear me talk of hunting in a childish sort of fashion,' he whispered. 'But the doing of it's another thing, eh? Is she ready? She still thinks it's a kind of pageant, a slice of fun. But I need her all grown up for the plans I have for us after this. She's got a lot of my strength inside her now, and I need all of it on my side to see my ambitions go fruitfully forward.

So, now, will you give us a worthwhile hunt, Elliott? Will you help me get her ready?'

Cullayn chuckled as he said that, leaning closer.

'Your father's in a bad way, son,' he tutted. 'We'll let him rest, shall we? But Janey, we'll not let her rest, no. She broke an oath to me. She was meant to bring you to me, but not hidden in the dark glamour she conjured. *I* bring the darkness here. So now I want that heart of hers bursting.' Cullayn stood. 'Therefore, let's set the terms of the hunt, the contest, the conditions. Eve will ensure all parties play honest and fair. I'll even give you a head start, boy. What time is it?'

'Five minutes to midnight!' Eve cried instantly.

'Five minutes to midnight.' Cullayn beamed. 'Fair enough. I'll give you till midnight then, Elliott. Five minutes to get lost and find yourself somewhere else. There's a way out. I've opened a door to outside no one knows about. If you can find it I'll let you go. By god, if you make it out I'll drag your father there myself, and Ben, and hand 'em back to you! I'll give you them both, your family entire. What do you say to that?'

Elliott stared at the star-eyes of Vincent Cullayn. A hint of truthfulness underlined his expression: he meant what he said. At the same time Elliott knew by now that Cullayn only made such an offer because he didn't expect to fail.

'You're right, boy,' Cullayn said, seeing his hesitation.

'I never lost a quarry before. Sam nearly outlasted me, but I got him in the end, and I'll get you as well.' He patted Elliott's shoulder amiably. 'I'll introduce you to my hunting ground soon, but first you've got to earn the right. We'll have a prior bit of a chase in the East Wing. Evey, are you ready?'

Eve stamped her feet. At first Elliott thought it was some kind of petulance, but then he saw it was a stamp of pride in Cullayn.

Cullayn clapped his hands, and all the daylight began to fade again.

'What … what about Janey?' Elliott managed to stutter, his heart sinking.

'The old dear gets to live as long as her legs can carry her,' Cullayn said indifferently, tugging at his beard. 'That old quailing bell of hers is already hammering away. If she falters on the hunt, I'll cut her down where she stands.'

Janey bent towards Elliott, hurriedly whispered, 'Just run. Even if I survive the East Wing, he'll kill me in the hunting ground, there's no escaping that now. I'll keep up as long as I can, lighting the way.'

'That's the spirit!' Cullayn said brightly, but he looked distracted now, wanting to begin. The darkness in the knight's room gradually became so complete that only the owner's starlit outline enabled Elliott to see anything at all. Cullayn's weapons rose up from the floor, and he juggled them, his feet dancing under him, his knees crossing back and forth too fast to see.

'Choose, choose, or get none!' he shouted wildly. 'I'll give you one weapon, Elliott, and in return I'll take nothing. How's that for an honest fight? Quick! Choose! Or I'll kill you.'

'A gun,' Elliott said immediately.

'Why?' Cullayn asked, still juggling. 'Scared of a knife? Scared to get so close?'

It was true. Elliott had been thinking he didn't want a close-quarter fight.

Cullayn roared with laughter. 'Then it's a gun, but since you did not ask for ammunition you may have to bludgeon me with it. Still, choices have been and will be honoured. Do you agree to the terms?'

'What if I refuse?'

'Then I'll strike you dead now,' Cullayn said bluntly. 'I'll have my hunt, if you please.'

Elliott reached for the gun. It vanished.

'A jest! Only our hands!' Cullayn cried, crackling with laughter, and Eve laughed with him. 'Should we give the boy some help?' Cullayn asked her. 'He looks so forlorn, poor lamb.'

'Yes!' Eve piped merrily.

'All right, all right, we will. What shall it be?' Cullayn made an exaggerated gesture of thinking deeply, drawing his fingers across his chin. Then he grinned, peering at

Eve. 'Let's show 'em how much you've learned under my artistic guidance, Evey. Make a spider-map!'

Eve nodded eagerly as Cullayn blew a puff of dust at her. She rapidly fashioned the particles into a delicate spiderweb-thin diagram depicting the East Wing. Adding details, sticking out her tongue in concentration, she handed it to Elliott.

The spider-map showed an exit somewhere behind him. But it was only a working of air and dust, never meant to last, and it was already crumbling in his fingers. He desperately tried to memorise the details.

'What time is it?' Cullayn thundered.

'Five minutes to midnight!' Eve yelled.

'So then! What's everyone waiting for?' Cullayn waggled his fingers. 'Tell him, Janey.'

Janey looked hard at Elliott.

'Run!' she said.

25

AS LIGHT AS
A SMALL GIRL

When every room, corridor, crease and tuck of air is your pursuer's vantage-point and trap, what do you do? Where do you go?

Elliott held the spider-map in front of his eyes and dashed back the way he had come. Janey raised her hand, illuminating the way. For two minutes she was able to pick up her legs at a fair pace and stay close enough to guide Elliott while he read the map. Left he went, right, straight on, and straight again, through a blur of rooms.

In Elliott's hands the dust-map disintegrated on draughts.

'I can't follow this!'

'Stop a minute, then!' Janey yelled, gasping for breath.

As Elliott paused the map's contours crumbled. He despairingly turned it this way and that.

'Do you have any idea where the exit is?' he said.

'No, but Cullayn won't be lying.'

'Where's the most likely place?'

As Janey chewed her lip, the remnants of the spider-map blew away.

'The rear of the East Wing,' she said, reading its dregs. 'Most of that borders the garden, not the house.' Already grey with tiredness Janey ran on, leading the way this time.

'You can't carry on at this pace,' Elliott told her.

Without slowing down, she said, 'I'm not going to live through this anyway. If I can help get you out of here, I will.'

They raced through the corridors. Elliott had no idea where he was: the carpets, the walls and intersections all looked the same. How long had it been since the hunt started? It doesn't matter, he realised. Cullayn decided the time here. *He* was the clock.

'One minute to midnight!' chirped a high voice behind them.

It was Eve, slipping in their wake so quietly that they'd been unaware of her.

'I am the timekeeper,' she announced. 'I ensure the fairness of the game. I am going back now to make sure Cullayn is still in the knight's room. I won't let him leave early, though he may wish to.' She gave Elliott a warm look, but he couldn't tell if she really meant him well or if she was just enjoying the whole experience of the chase as much as Cullayn.

'Eve,' Janey said, trembling with fatigue. 'Do you ...
do you know the way out?'

She nodded.

'Won't you show us?'

'I can't do that. It's against the rules.'

'They're Cullayn's rules, and we should not live by
them,' Janey told her.

'Shouldn't we?'

'No, there are other rules. Better ones. Better games.
We can take you out of here. Don't you want us to?'

Eve rolled her eyes as if Janey had just said the funniest
thing in the world. 'You have one minute left,' she said.
'I'll hold him back till midnight. I'll try, anyway.' She
smiled fiercely at them both, raising her fists to remind
them to get ready. Then, with Janey pleading with her
to come back, Eve flitted back into the dark in a flurry
of dust.

Elliott watched her go. Above Janey's head a portrait
of Cullayn gazed down at him with unending acquisitive
interest.

'This way,' Janey groaned.

Elliott had no idea how she kept going. She pressed
him on, one corridor after another, a snaking,
horrendously complex route that took them gradually
towards the back end of the East Wing. Finally they
reached a wall where the corridor could go no further
forward, only right and left. They were in the correct

area, and ran frantically back and forth searching for the exit.

Moments later, they heard a clock tick. Then Eve's small voice began counting down from ten. A boom like a futile bell clanged in time with her countdown, matching it, underlining it, and on the final brutal chime Cullayn's confident voice rumbled a distant, resonant, 'Midnight!'

Elliott glanced at Janey. Her face held no answers.

From the heart of the East Wing behind them came a huge breath of stale wind. It ricocheted past their faces, stretching their cheeks.

'I am coming! I am on my way to you!' Cullayn bellowed, his words issuing from all directions at once.

Janey lay down in a crumpled heap on the floor, utterly spent. 'Go on!' she rasped. 'I'll keep Cullayn here as long as I can.'

'No,' Elliott said, and before Janey knew what he was doing he'd lifted her onto his shoulder. She was as light as a girl. She tried to protest, but she didn't even have the breath left for that, and Elliott didn't waste time with talk of his own. Adjusting Janey's weight on his back, he ran. From the limits of exhaustion Janey raised two fingers, enough to light the way for a dozen more corridors. Then even that light started to fade.

Panting for breath himself, unable to see a thing, Elliott's feet faltered in the darkness. But Cullayn did not come, and after another minute he still did not come. And then Janey's finger-light finally guttered out, and only then did Elliott understand why Cullayn had delayed. Of course. He'd been waiting until Janey had nothing left. Janey had to know that she'd failed Elliott before Cullayn dispatched her.

Abruptly daylight was allowed back into the corridors, and Elliott sensed it was because Cullayn wanted him to see Janey's exhausted face.

Janey protested for Elliott to go on without her. She clawed at his back until he laid her down, on her side. By a chink of ceiling light he could see how drained her face was. 'I can't go on,' she said. 'But you must. He'll stop here first to gloat. That'll give you at least a couple more minutes. Use them.'

'But—'

'No, enough. I'm dead already. Get out if you can.'

'Wait,' Elliott said, thinking furiously. 'What if I give you time to recover? Get Cullayn away from you? Maybe that way he'll ignore you, and you can get back to Dad and Ben – get them out by the main entrance. Do you know where they are?'

'Yes.' Janey opened her hand, allowing a splinter of light to spill between her fingers – a final moment of brightness between them. 'A chase, then? One to lead Cullayn away?' She hesitated, turning the idea over in her mind. 'Even that might not distract him enough.

But ...' She felt for Elliott's hand. 'All right, brave boy. Go now! Run and don't stop. Give him his hunt! And I'll do my best to rescue your family.'

Elliott stood, preparing himself. He took three deep breaths and then yelled at the top of his voice to get Cullayn's attention. He wasn't sure he'd drawn the owner's focus away from Janey until he heard feet bounding into an adjacent corridor.

The hunt was on.

Shuddering, Elliott tore down three corridors, using clefts of ceiling light to steer him.

Cullayn made no attempt to hide his pursuit. He came one moment in a thumping slog, a giant's terrifying stamp, in the next light and elf-swift and full of bubbling, hummed tunes.

'Too easy! Too easy!' came his close cry, adrift in its own joy. 'Too timid! Is this all you've got to offer?' Twin beams of white light lanced into the rich red of the carpet ahead of Elliott. He turned to see Cullayn's eyes glowing like strips of polished new mirror. 'Come on!' Cullayn roared. 'Don't make this too simple for me! I'll kill Ben if you do! I'll kill him anyway, but I'll kill him slowly. Give me a good hunt and I'll make it quick!'

Elliott launched himself forward again. Two intersections later he blundered into a large fragment of wood. He realised at once that it was the same improvised weapon Dad had carried inside the East

Wing. Cullayn had obviously deliberately left it for Elliott as a reminder of what had happened to his father. With nothing else on offer, Elliott picked it up anyway. He tested using the fragment as a knife.

A sigh of warm approval came from behind him.

Elliott ran on. Kicking open the doors off the corridors, he searched for a better weapon. In one bedroom he found a fireplace. He felt his way around the grate and his fingers finally came across a metal poker. Throwing the piece of wood down, Elliott tested to see if he could handle the poker. This time a definite snort of appreciation came from behind him in the corridor.

I'm just helping him enjoy this more, Elliott realised. But that, after all, was what Janey needed. That was OK. Let Cullayn bask in his enjoyment if it gave Janey time to get to Dad and Ben.

The poker was useless. Too heavy. He could only swish it in a wide circle. Picking the wooden fragment up again, Elliott ran on, experimenting with grips.

He threw himself into a long corridor. All the doors off it were closed, but he pushed them wide, hoping to confuse Cullayn. Redoubling his efforts, he flung himself forward, smashing into walls and running on, the only thought in his mind being to keep the hunter's voice behind him. That voice came as a series of intermittent, happy roars.

Cullayn lingered in the long corridor, but not for long.

Elliott thrust recklessly on, extraordinarily tired now. His one hope was that he might blunder accidentally across the East Wing's main entrance, and have a chance to get into the garden. He was turning into another corridor, with Cullayn crowing with excitement behind him, when his temple struck a jutting wall.

With his skull ringing from the impact, Elliott slumped to the carpet. Swaying, he raised his face. He was in a place where the floor descended. Ahead of him was a small set of steps.

'Dad! Ben!' Elliott yelled, sensing that if they were anywhere it was here.

Then he shushed himself, pressed away from the dark passageway. What was he doing? He had to give Janey *more time* to get to Ben and Dad, not lead Cullayn to them. 'Come on then!' he yelled back over his shoulder, deciding that if he was going to be caught anyway he might as well insult Cullayn instead of always being the one taunted. 'Where are you, old man?'

'Good!' Cullayn yelled. 'You promised me a fight! You promised!' The voice was a child's spoilt whine, but it was also gleeful, delighted, excited and looking for Elliott's death.

Hearing it, Elliott knew beyond any doubt that Cullayn would kill him as soon as he stopped being an interesting enough chase.

Above Elliott there was a triangle of glass. Smash it, he thought. The ghost children must still be out there somewhere. He rammed the shard of wood into the glass. The glass shattered. Air burst inside and for a moment Cullayn's roar lessened. Then, when it was obvious the ghost children were not coming through, his voice swelled with confidence again.

Elliott hurled himself on. He dived into rooms, kicked past furniture, jumped over beds. He threw himself down corridors, and all the while, behind him, he could hear Cullayn. He was imitating Elliott between bouts of laughter, pretending to be tired, huffing and puffing.

Elliott was now beginning to feel physically sick with exhaustion. But he didn't let that slow him down. Sheer tiredness meant he kept bumping into walls, tripping and falling, but he was beyond caring. He let his anger fuel him, let the burning ache of Cullayn's voice pitch him headlong into the darkness.

When he did eventually rest a moment, he dared for the first time in several minutes to look behind.

Cullayn was there, of course. But he had changed – from the growling monster into the silent pursuer. He looked like something mythic: a silhouette outlined in streaming white starlight against the dark grey of the corridor.

Elliott pushed himself onward again. Every part of

him was sore from working so hard to stay in front, but he was slowing. And suddenly, with a sigh that might have been contentment, Cullayn's star-studded back rose against the wall of the corridor ahead of Elliott. The wall was utterly engulfed by shadow as Cullayn reared up like a wave, and Elliott closed his eyes, waiting for the impact.

When that impact did not come Elliott leapt forward again, but his heel slipped on the carpet, his knee slamming into the floor. He sat up immediately, suppressing a yell as he flexed his leg to test the damage. At the same time he gazed back to see how close Cullayn was. The answer showed him that the chase was finally over.

Cullayn had assumed a heroic pose. He was in fanciful flight, a mid-air lunge, his boots on the rise, his head thrown back. Snatching his hat aloft in triumph, he licked the fingertips of his weapon-hand and his mouth became a shout of delight, a raw crescendo that made the carpet and walls vibrate. Elliott braced himself and the air felt suddenly ice-cold. Cruising overhead, Cullayn lifted Elliott with one colossally strong arm and held him high and then higher still. In that moment Cullayn fully intended to kill Elliott. He wanted to, would have done, except that he had waited so long and so keenly to hunt anything at all that instead of grinding Elliott's life into the carpet fibres he decided to postpone the final hunt for later.

As Elliott tensed for the impact, Cullayn laughed, crushing the side of Elliott's head. Elliott felt his cheek shatter and break, and a wave of pain washed over him that briefly left him unconscious.

When he woke again a few seconds later, Cullayn was sitting beside him. The hunter looked calm. He looked happy. A fulfilled gleam gladdened his eye as he fondly ruffled Elliott's hair. 'I'm going after Janey now,' he said. 'I delayed that pleasure, as I did your death, and now I'm glad I did both.' Looking pleased with himself, he flowed down the corridor.

As Elliott watched him, he knew that Cullayn could catch up with Janey without having to run. His strides could be as wide as he liked without him seeming to hurry.

Feeling the broken bones in his face, Elliott staggered away. But Cullayn was soon back. The owner of Glebe House sat against a corridor wall ahead of him, breathing lightly and easily.

'Thank you,' he said in all sincerity, once Elliott could focus on him. 'I have not had such a chase since Sam. And as reward, because I am not an unreasonable man . . .' Cullayn traced a doorway with his finger.

There it was, no more than a footstep away: a path into the grounds. Outside was freedom: trees, sunshine, birds and ghosts. The ghost children floated in the sky. They had been following the progress of the hunt from outside. Elliott could only see them because he and they were so close to Cullayn. They stirred with concern for him and the others within.

'Ah, Elliott, they'd love to get in here with me and have a chase of their own,' Cullayn said with satisfaction. 'But they're too scared, as they've always been.'

He sat next to Elliott, comradely. 'You know,' Cullayn said in a quiet, sated tone, 'it's a whole world out there. I've missed it to be honest. Missed my slope, yes, missed my hunting ground, but maybe I stayed here overlong. I got too comfortable in Glebe House. That's how I got caught. But at least when your brother's dead I'll have all that extra energy for myself. I can pack it inside me, squirrel it away.' Cullayn sniffed, patting Elliott's shoulder in an almost fatherly way. 'Good, good,' he said. 'I'm glad you're paying attention. Because what's the point of fine plans with no one to share the wonder of them, eh? See, Elliott, truth is, I want to bring the hunt everywhere. When Ben's dead I'll have enough energy to make a start, and following that I'll drain Janey as well. I'll do her last of all. Her spirit won't go quick like the rest of the adults. She's different. And then I'll go right through this door you see before us – right out into the garden and beyond.'

Cullayn snapped his fingers, laughed. 'See, I've

planned my exit, Elliott. It'll have some poetry, I promise you that. I intend to stop a moment to smell the garden fragrances, something small and trivial and innocent like that, something Janey might have done to comfort the ghost children. And then, do you remember that white steed beneath the knight? That impressive horse? Well, that will be me. I'll pass like Pegasus himself over the gathered ghost-children. They probably won't even try to stop me, they're such weak wretches, but even if they do it'll be too late. With Ben and Janey inside me I'll outfly them, soar over them, and they'll be left behind knowing that they stayed here all this time for nought. That'll be something worth dwelling over, won't it? That's an exit!'

Cullayn stood, smiling. 'Anyway, I don't really need you, that's what I'm coming to in this little chat. Ben and Janey are enough. You can go.' He gazed down at Elliott. 'Well? What are you waiting for? I never make an offer twice.'

Elliott didn't move. He knew by now there must be conditions attached.

Cullayn laughed. 'I like you, Elliott. You haven't whined yet. That's what's kept you alive, not your speed. So then, here's the charity I'm offering. Leave freely now, or try to make it back to my secret room. That's where your father and Ben are. They're both still alive. The room's not far from here. It's never far from wherever you are in here, eh? And if you make it there before me, I'll let you all go. I promise. I'll even free Janey. Oh yes,' Cullayn said, when he saw Elliott's eyes widen. 'I caught her. 'Course I did.'

'What if I don't get there before you?'

Cullayn grinned good-naturedly. 'Do you really need to ask that?'

Elliott shook his head.

'That's it, then,' Cullayn said, tightening his belt. 'I've given you plenty of chances, Elliott, and so far you've not availed yourself of any. What do you say to a gallant ending? Or do you just want to leave? Take my first offer? Save your skin?'

Cullayn flicked his hand towards the opening into the garden – a you-may-go gesture. Elliott could hear singing birds out there. He could smell the grass Dad had mown yesterday. He turned to face Cullayn.

'Excellent!' Cullayn rasped, seeing the decision he had made. 'Good boy! No wonder your father's so proud of you. Let's make him even prouder, eh?'

'No tricks if I race you back to the passage?' Elliott said, knowing how pointless a question it was.

Cullayn's eyes twinkled. 'I can't promise that.'

'I want a head start.'

'I'll bet you do. I'll give you one minute. I've already given you more time than you deserve.'

'My leg's broken,' Elliott said, finding it hard to speak

because of his shattered cheek. 'What kind of contest is it unless you give me a fair start?' He rose, testing his swelling left knee. The ligaments pulled, knifing pain up his thigh, but nothing was broken. He'd lied, hoping to gain a few more seconds. And another thing: he didn't remember much about the spider-map, but he thought he recalled the details of how to get back to the dark passageway.

'Broken?' Cullayn tutted disinterestedly. 'You'll have to hop, then. A man did that once, a sort of hobble to get away from me.' He stood up to show Elliott what it had looked like.

Elliott practised the gait once, and limp-strode up the corridor.

As soon as he was out of sight, he ran as hard as he could. Three teeth on the left side of his jaw felt loose, but he ignored the pain, desperately trying to recall the details of the spider-map. Time passed – a haze of minutes – and suddenly Elliott felt the corridor descending.

There it was, ahead of him: the small set of steps.

Elliott lunged forward.

Only to find Cullayn jauntily trotting beside him.

'Amazingly, you *did* go the right way,' Cullayn said. 'That poor broken leg must hurt. Let me give you a hand.'

He lifted Elliott roughly by the scruff of the neck,

hauling him into the narrow dark passageway.

'See this?' Cullayn said, opening a concealed door in the wall. 'It hid me when they came to string me up. Came for a hanging they did, and got diddly-squat.' Cullayn showed Elliott the absence of rope-marks on his neck. 'By the way, you failed, boy. Time's up. You're mine now, your life's forfeit, and you'll watch your father die before Ben sees me despatch you on the hunting ground.'

The wall opened fully. Cullayn threw Elliott inside and jumped in after him, drawing the door shut.

26

THE DARK PASSAGE

Inside, Elliott saw several things at once. He saw Ben kneeling on the stone floor. He saw Dad lying on his side, barely conscious. And he saw Janey. She sat stiffly against a wall, looking as if she was about to have a heart attack – or was holding one at bay only by force of will.

From Ben's inconsolable expression, Elliott could tell that whatever influence Cullayn had once had on him was relinquished. Of course it was. Cullayn didn't need that version of Ben any longer. He wanted him as frightened as everyone else.

Elliott limped across. It was hard to believe how much blood from Dad's head was pooled on the floor. After making him as comfortable as he could, Elliott hunkered down next to Ben and whispered in his ear, 'Are you all right?'

Ben nodded tightly, containing his fear. 'Look what's behind you.'

Elliott turned. Inevitably a large portrait of Cullayn

dominated the view. Even in this most secret of rooms Cullayn hadn't been able to resist decorating the walls with images of himself. This particular portrait, however, was unique. It showed the owner in smiling close-up but, behind him, the hunting ground was victimless. No one was on the slope. Considering that, Elliott wondered why he found the portrait so disturbing.

Then he understood. It was the very emptiness of the slope.

'It's waiting for *us*,' Ben said, having had more time to take in the significance of the painting. 'We're next.'

'My favourite bit of artwork,' Cullayn remarked, noticing Elliott's stare. 'Has a certain vigour, wouldn't you say?'

The owner had discarded his starry outline, and now stood before them in straightforward hunting leathers. He glanced briefly at Dad. 'Your father can't last much longer, boys,' he grunted. 'I doubt this is the fate he envisaged for himself. When he strode so manfully into my East Wing I bet he saw himself as a soldier guarding both his sons from everything wicked. As for the hag' – Cullayn jerked a thumb at Janey – 'her nightmare was always that she'd be the one to help me broaden my hunt. And now she's done just that, hasn't she? I could never have fetched you both in here half so neatly without her.'

Janey looked pitiful – breathing raggedly, head lowered. Cullayn bent down to her, pretended to caress her face, then slapped it. She offered no reaction.

Strewn across the floor were the remains of three dead bodies. One was the owner. Cullayn's ghost had rearranged his own desiccated skeleton in a perky pose: arms folded, head on one side, his dead eye sockets gazing wistfully up at his own painted hunting ground.

The other two skeletons were the remains of Theo and Eve. Their clothes, including Eve's red dress, still clung to their collapsed bodies. Theo's arms were around Eve's shoulders, still holding onto her after all these years.

'Touching, isn't it?' Cullayn said tonelessly. Now that the hunt was temporarily suspended, he looked bored. 'Oh, why wait?' he muttered to Elliott. 'I was toying with letting you and Janey have a break, so you'd give me a longer fight, but what do you say? Ready for the hunting ground?'

'Don't make the others go to the knight's room,' Janey said, coming to life. 'Don't make them have to watch.'

Cullayn laughed – obviously happy that Janey had helped him make up his mind – and without bothering to answer her he plucked Dad and Ben effortlessly up from the floor, one in each hand. 'No rest for you either, my dear,' he said to Janey. 'C'mon.'

Cullayn led the way from the secret room down a series of twisting corridors, watching Janey's cheeks puff crimson. 'You were wrong about why Eve likes the knight's room, by the way,' he told her conversationally. 'It's not because she wants to be rescued. She likes that room because it's the gateway to the hunting ground. There's a lovely view, a fine perspective of the slope and trees. She can't wait to get started, can you, Evey?'

Eve did not answer, but Elliott could see the eagerness in her eyes.

Cullayn hurried them ever faster along the corridors. They finally reached the knight's room. Eve dutifully closed the door behind them.

All this time Elliott had been searching for a way to distract Cullayn, give Ben at least a chance to get out. But he hadn't been able to think of anything, and once they were inside the knight's room what little chance there might have been seemed gone.

Rubbing his hands in anticipation, Cullayn sauntered across to the window overlooking the slope. He peered out.

Eve paid no attention to anyone once she entered the room. She was more interested in the knight. She kept staring devotedly at it, tilting her head curiously. Only

Elliott was watching as she suddenly pulled back. Eve frowned. Twitching her shoulders, she gazed at the scene afresh, as if puzzled by a difference she was not expecting.

It was only then that Elliott caught Janey's glance – a knowing glint in her old eye. A sly look that said *stay quiet*, and made him turn back to the knight.

'The best place to hide a book is in a library,' Janey murmured so only he could hear. 'The best place to hide from the hunter is in his lair.' Elliott stared at her blankly. 'In the visible angle,' Janey whispered. 'In plain sight, in view.' She gave a definite nod of acknowledgment towards the tapestry. Then she unobtrusively pulled her thin legs from under her so that she could rise when she had to, and cracked the joints in her fingers.

Elliott saw that she'd kept something in reserve after all.

'I knew Cullayn wouldn't kill me in the East Wing,' she whispered. 'I knew he'd dally, want to play first before he put me on his slope. How could he resist? I needed to watch him fight – the hunter in action. As a teenage girl I'd seen evidence of that, but memory's unreliable, and anyway he was bound to have added a few new wrinkles to his technique. I had to delay until I saw what he could do. And now I've seen exactly what that is.'

She gave Elliott a guarded smile. 'You were right about Theo,' she murmured. 'I knew he'd stay close to Eve if he could, watch over her. But where was he? It took me a long time to work out why Eve kept coming to the knight's room. It has nothing to do with the view over the hunting ground. She doesn't even know herself what draws her. But Theo kept himself in the one place Cullayn wouldn't think to look. Cullayn would never think to look for a ghost that *stayed still*.'

Eve kept blinking at the knight. She ran her fingers over its brow. She picked at the helmet, prodded the armour. Then she let out a sudden cough of sheer surprise – and stepped back.

At the same time a shocked Ben peered up at the knight and Janey abruptly stood up. Flexing her wrists, she began a concentrated slow-breathing.

Cullayn turned back from the window – surprised but not yet alarmed.

From partially-shut eyes, Dad managed to glance up. He felt a static electrical charge building up fast in the room. It puckered his skin. As he blearily searched for the source of it, wondering if it was a new threat to his sons, the life-sized knight began to move.

A stitch – a simple dash of cotton – stretched.

Slowly it expanded, and out of the intricate needlework, caked in threads of cotton, a pattern surfaced – a shape. It was hidden for a moment in the embroidery making up the knight's stark outline.

Then Eve screamed when she saw who it was.

Cullayn ran towards Eve, but it was Theo's ghost – detaching himself, flinging the fibres of cotton from his ghost form – who reached her sooner.

The first thing Theo did was to gaze fearlessly at Cullayn to hold him back. The second was to bring Eve into his arms and kiss her on the cheek so that she knew he was real.

As she gasped in astonishment, Theo turned quickly to Janey.

'I knew you'd come,' he murmured.

'I'm very late,' she apologised. 'But you know I had to wait for Eve. Until enough of Cullayn's power was inside her.'

'I know,' Theo said, smiling. 'Are you ready?'

'Yes.'

Janey curled her fingers – a supple rotation of the tips – and abruptly the air tightened around her. She peered over her brows at Cullayn and with her gnarled fingers swept a shape around him that was rectangular.

Cullayn, who in that moment had been a blur of speed lunging towards Theo to smash him, found his hand ... held.

He looked at it in surprise, the way it disobeyed. Then

he stared with renewed respect at Janey and smiled to disarm her, but the smile had none of his characteristic poise, and they all saw that. Cullayn tried using his other hand. Janey mirrored his movement with her own. Cullayn kicked out at Theo. Janey raised an ankle, stopping him.

'Eve,' Theo said softly. She'd stepped back from him, an arm's length of astonishment. Theo held both his hands out to her.

She hesitated – looked between him and Cullayn.

Taking strength from that hesitation, Cullayn began contorting his body. He flung himself about – different combinations – attempting to find a way out of Janey's hold. Finally, by jerking a hand, knee and elbow simultaneously, she failed to stop one of Cullayn's booted feet and it connected.

But not with Theo. Ben and Elliott had stepped in front of him to take the blow. Knocked backwards, the brothers were hurled across the floor.

Cullayn grunted in anger, but his limbs were freer now. 'So, you're not quite the perfect puppeteer after all,' he said to Janey.

He twisted his body and Janey – a study in concentration – almost matched him. But not quite. 'Hurry,' she whispered to Theo. 'I can't hold him like this for long. Do something.'

'Not me,' Theo said.

He turned to Eve. She blinked back at him, confused.

'Eve,' Cullayn growled, his whole body in motion. 'Kill Janey.'

Elliott threw himself across the floor to defend Janey as best he could, and Ben joined him.

Eve stared at Cullayn, clearly wanting to obey the master of Glebe House. But Theo's eyes held her, too. Wavering, she comfort-snatched Katerina up from the floor, pressed the doll to her cheek.

'You left me!' she shrieked at Theo. 'You left me!'

Cullayn continued to writhe to free himself from Janey's restraints.

'I never left you,' Theo explained, tears in his eyes. 'I was always here. I had to wait. I couldn't ever let him see me. But I was here, watching over you. And now it's time to go.'

'No!' Eve said. Events, choices she had to make, were moving too fast for her. She clutched herself through her dress, and in that terrible moment of indecision Elliott knew that Cullayn had truly lodged the hope of the everlasting hunt in her heart, and everything hung in the balance.

'Eve!' Cullayn's voice was rich and warm. With a great shriek he part-broke from Janey's control, lunging at Theo.

Janey made a triangle of three fingers and *clicked* them

hard together, stopping Cullayn in mid-lunge. Making a fist of her hand, she blocked, pushed and bent back his arm. At the same time Theo formed a circle with his hands and squeezed it towards Cullayn, hemming him in.

Snarling, unable to make his blow count, Cullayn studied Janey intently, observing how her control techniques worked. As he gradually did so, Elliott saw that Cullayn was the stronger of the two. In fact, he was stronger than any combination of her and Theo. And suddenly Cullayn must have sensed that, too, because he changed tactics. Using one jutting fist after another he punched the air, thrusting out, hitting nothing except emptiness, but weakening Janey.

Eve watched – horrified, mesmerised. Her wide-eyed expression was lodged somewhere between awe and disbelief, but there was also soul-searching there. For a moment she looked at Ben, and it was simply a young girl looking at the child closest to her own age for advice about what she should do. Ben stared resolutely back at her, and stood closer to Elliott.

Outside the window three ghosts hovered. They were so near to Cullayn that Elliott could see their outlines.

'Smash the window!' Janey yelled desperately at him. 'Let them in!'

'No!' roared Cullayn. He raised a fist to flatten Elliott.

Then he gazed down in curiosity as that fist was held again. Not this time by a barrier erected by Janey, however. It was Eve who held it. She possessed so much of Cullayn's power, and now she gave him an arch look that he knew as his own.

'I watched you with her,' Theo said to Cullayn with cold deliberation. 'I watched everything. You taught her well.'

'Eve, please ...' It was an astonishing moment. Cullayn pleading. Eve held his fist and he pleaded and, because she was still partly his creature, his weakness was enough to end any doubt in her mind, and she gripped him tighter than ever and looked fiercely at Elliott.

'Do it!' she told him.

Elliott dragged his injured knee across the room. Using an elbow, helped by Ben, he smashed the window.

Outside it was a warm, calm summer morning. Three figures came through that calm – ending it.

Sam was the first to blast past Elliott and Ben. He came so fast that he knocked both brothers aside and placed himself in front of Cullayn, raising his arms. Nell and Alice came next, taking up a determined position left and right of the owner, bracketing him.

Cullayn looked between them, wavering between fighting tactics. Leo was holding back, floating alone beyond the window. He was still too afraid to come inside. All those centuries ago too much had happened to him. Even Eve could see that, how torn he was. But at least he stood his ground outside, and when Cullayn bared his teeth at him, with a shiver Leo managed to whisper, '*L is for Leo, who gave his all*,' hissing Cullayn's own verse back to him at last.

Eve gasped when she heard that. She put one hand to her mouth, and when Cullayn tried to answer Leo back she tightened her other hand on the owner's wrist until he squealed. That squeal brought movement. Suddenly the ghosts were all on the move. They came at Cullayn, they were all over him, Alice and Nell on his back, Theo pinning him down, Eve holding his arms still while Janey stood and wrenched the air around Cullayn's spine, restricting his motion. And finally, bursting through the window with a yell, Leo joined them.

Cullayn's limbs were restrained as one by one Eve and the ghost children clambered on top of him, and though he kept throwing them off they always came back, until eventually Cullayn was exhausted and Janey was able to relax her efforts and collapse on the floor.

At the same moment Theo bent down, and it was to kiss Eve.

She seemed surprised, and suddenly she sobbed, and

to the sound of that Cullayn was dragged by the ghost children to the shattered window. There was something fresh and wonderful about the ghosts as they did so. Elliott, Ben and Dad could see them clearly now. It was not only Cullayn's power but their own that illuminated them.

They hauled the owner of Glebe House across the knight's room and out, out towards the slope. Elliott and Ben stumbled as best they could to the window as Cullayn was taken to the foot of the hunting ground. Janey managed to heave herself from the floor as well and, assisted by Ben, Elliott got Dad to his feet, holding him up so that they could all take in the view.

Cullayn was carried onto his slope. From the base of it he stared up at the distant woods. The ghost children encircled him. Visible in flashes, their own light colours competed against Cullayn's darker flecks of orange and red. With the others gripping him tightly, Sam took Cullayn by the scruff of the neck. Holding him like a dog, he gazed back at Dad.

'Say it,' he spat. 'Say it!'

Dad nodded, his measured gaze meeting Cullayn's.

'Run,' he said.

Cullayn did not immediately do so. His still-calculating mind roved, assessing the children, not quite believing they would chase him. Then he looked at Eve.

They all did. And for a moment her cold eyes were utterly the owner's again, and Cullayn understood: it didn't matter if the other children did not start the hunt. If they were too scared to set the first foot on the slope to begin the chase, Eve would.

Never taking her eyes off Cullayn, she raised a single foot – and with a small jump, Cullayn scuttled off.

He looked over his shoulder as he ran. It was a new experience for the owner, to be looking backward instead of forward on that slope. A rise of about two hundred metres was in front of him, in ruts of mud and meadow-grass. The ghost children watched him race towards the trees as intensely as anything has ever watched anything, but they did not chase him.

Two thirds of the way to the wood Cullayn turned to see their lack of pursuit.

'I knew you'd be too afraid to come after me,' he crowed. 'I knew—'

A wind struck his cheek, interrupting him. Cullayn swatted idly at it. 'I told you—' The wind struck him again, harder, knocking him off his feet.

Bewildered, intensely frightened, Cullayn tried to see who was there.

Nobody. No one. But not nothing. A living presence seethed against him. A hunter of Cullayn's own creation had arrived.

Even from here Elliott could feel the lacerating aura

of the hunting ground. The trees shivered, seemed to inhale a vast and unseen collective breath and, hearing it, the ghost children fled back to the knight's room. Cullayn was still staggering sideways on the slope, trying to stay upright, when the hunting ground came for him. He'd kept it waiting, and though it was only trees and a patch of land when he was not on it, with his arrival it was *his* appetite it shared, and now it was impatient. Abandoning all restraint in the same way Cullayn himself had done so often, the land came for him.

Inside the knight's room everyone – young and old, alive and dead – instinctively held each other. Janey put her arms around the ghost children, as naturally a part of them as she had always been.

Outside, the leaves of the massed trees heaved. Many shapes they formed, framed by branches. Only Cullayn recognised those shapes, because they dwelled entirely and solely in his own nightmares. It was all a game being played, just a game – one of Cullayn's very own – but even the best games have to end. And finally the hunting ground chose that end. It selected the longest path a wounded victim had ever had to crawl on Cullayn's slope, and, in a final heart-stopping shriek it did not even allow the owner to complete, it made him dance along it until he was gone.

It was over. The trees stilled, relaxing into themselves

again. Birds rose skyward, their beaks dipped in silence. Beneath them, the cleansed oak trees, dappled in sunshine, wrapped themselves in evening dew.

27

A MILDEWED BENCH

A week later, once the worst of Dad's injuries were mending, and Elliott's cheekbone had been set, and everyone living and dead could do so, they gathered in the warmth of a late summer evening in September on the western lawns of the Glebe estate.

The western lawns were the finest of the venerable old property. Glebe House had possessed gardens long before Cullayn arrived, and they had been laid by people who loved to grow things, and though the grass was now patchy and waist-high, tree saplings sprouting everywhere, and most of the garden ornaments falling to pieces (Dad still hadn't found a single one of the gnomes), the quality of the original landscape gardeners' vision remained. Never more so than to the ghost children. They had witnessed the grounds in their golden years, and remembered them that way still.

It was a sultry day. Summer cumulous had built all afternoon in the heat haze, but now the sky was a smooth ceramic blue.

Elliott stood with the others. With sleeves rolled up, he stared at the East Wing, giving it his full attention.

Something special was about to happen. Dad had managed to persuade the owners of Glebe House that the East Wing was an eyesore that reduced the estate's value. The owners were only interested in selling it, and when he offered to take care of the problem for a modest fee a deal was done.

To bring down a building Dad normally used a straightforward wrecking ball. He'd been toying with something economical and sensible like that for the East Wing as well, but he was glad when both Ben and Elliott came to him early in the planning stage to request something slightly more spectacular.

'I want it to be exactly like a bomb going off,' Ben said.

'Yeah, it needs to be impressive,' Elliott agreed. 'Flames. Lots of flames. Portraits on fire flying out of the building, that sort of thing.'

'Mm,' Dad mused. 'Of course I'll have to place the portraits on the outer walls to create that effect. But I guess that's not impossible. Any more requests?'

Ben beamed. 'I want to be the one who blows it up.'

'You OK with that?' Dad asked Elliott.

'Sure,' Elliott said. 'As long as I can drive the tractor that wrecks its foundations.'

'It's illegal for you to drive a piece of machinery like that,' Dad told him. 'You're underage. Unless ...' he pretended to sort through papers ' ... I've somehow got your date of birth wrong.'

'You have,' Elliott said. 'I'm legal to drive anything. I'm seventeen.'

Dad peered at the East Wing, then back at Elliott. He gazed at his son's cheek, still full of temporary pins holding it together.

'Yes,' he said. 'You are.'

*

It was an enormous pleasure for Janey, assisted by Elliott, to hoist the hydraulic drill up to her shoulder and punch the first holes into the East Wing's walls for the explosives. A demolition team then rigged the building to blow, using special shaped charges to make sure it did not damage the main house.

The last act was to carefully remove the tapestry of the knight. Elliott undertook this with Janey, and they were watched as they did so by Eve and Theo. Like the other ghost children they had stayed behind, and for the last few days Janey had been their go-between in many conversations with the living. At first talks were halting as everyone felt their way towards an understanding despite all the years between them, but they soon got over that, and now there was nothing the children, living and dead, did not know about each other.

With the sun now hanging low in the sky, Ben stood beside the plunger, gripping the handle. Theo, Eve and the other children were next to him, adding ghostly weight to his hand. The plunger was linked by neat wires to explosive devices. They were only waiting to be triggered.

Dad gave Janey the nod. Smiling, she wiped a grey curl out of her eyes, and quietly said, '*Now.*'

Seven sets of hands lowered the plunger.

For a moment nothing happened. It looked as though the signal to the charges had been jammed, and everyone collectively held their breaths.

Then they picked up the internal *crump* of the first detonations. It was one of the most beautiful sounds any of them had ever heard.

Milliseconds later the entire front portion of the East Wing blasted into the sky.

'Whoa!' Ben cried, as hundreds of the owner's portraits spewed outward in three directions, sheets of fire ripping through their canvases, and for one glorious and surreal moment the air was loaded with the tang of ancient linseed oil, paint and preservative fluids.

Then came the furniture. In a great blaze curtains burned, bathroom mirrors cracked and beds roasted in their own linen. Unseen by any of them, the East Wing's rich burgundy carpet blackened and fused to the floorboards. The brass handles, clinging to the doors, began to melt.

No one could take their eyes from the destruction. Ben stood there, his hand still on the plunger, with Elliott and Janey beside him, and all around them the sky turned a dirty, indistinct orange. But it was not over yet. Dad had arranged a finale. Ten late charges detonated, and suddenly the corridor walls, which had held so many prisoners inside the East Wing, imploded and then *exploded*. Sparks burst up like swarms of fireflies through the gaps, and with a shivering *whoosh* the roof collapsed.

For two or three perfect minutes it was like the middle of the night as a pall of reeking smoke rose up and up. Then, with tongues of flame still curling inside the ruin of the East Wing, it was over.

*

Everyone turned away from the destruction. Instead, they looked at Eve. Elliott realised that she was trying to mouth *sorry* to them all. But the time for apologies was over. Janey pressed her hand, and it was Janey, not anyone else, who, opening her arms, said to all the ghost children, 'And now you can go.'

They gazed at her, blinking uncertainly. It wasn't an easy thing Janey was asking. Alice, Leo, Nell and Sam had been here for so much time that they had almost forgotten what was waiting for them on the other side.

'It's all right,' Janey said. 'Didn't I say that if we waited for long enough something wonderful would happen?'

The ghost children smiled. There was no sense of being rushed. There was time for embracing and for kisses. And then, once they were ready, it was Sam Cosgrove who took the lead. He rose up, high over the burning remnants of the East Wing, and made a long, slow circle over what had been the hunting ground. Now that Cullayn was gone the slope and the trees had returned to what they had been all along: a beautiful wooded upland, a place for butterflies and meadow-grass.

For a few minutes the other ghost children watched Sam flying overhead. Then Alice, Leo and Nell joined him and the four of them drew together, holding hands in a line and disappearing one at a time quietly over the horizon.

Theo and Eve remained. There was an awkward moment when no one knew what to say.

'What do you want us to do with your diary?' Ben asked at last, and everyone laughed.

'Publish it,' Theo said, grinning. 'Thank you,' he said to them all and, beside him, Eve nodded, clutching her brother's arm tighter.

Elliott took a deep breath and stepped forward. As he did so he automatically put out his arm to shake Theo's hand, then realised he couldn't. Theo laughed, raised his own hand in a half-salute instead, and glanced behind him.

Something was beckoning. A warm gusting wind.

'It's OK,' Janey said in the softest of voices to Theo. 'You really can leave, you know. If you're ready.'

At that, Theo nodded to her, and suddenly the breeze that was not from the garden became stronger and wilder, stirring his hair. Feeling it, the living stepped back, knowing its passion was not for them. But, before the wind could take Theo, Janey couldn't help herself – she rushed into his arms. She kissed him and he kissed her old, wrinkled face back, and they held each other, and something was said between them that would always be theirs alone.

Then Theo suddenly laughed, picked Eve up and whirled her round. As she rose from the ground Theo caught her hand and, never letting go of it, led her away across the grass. They walked at first, and then a breeze picked them up and they drifted quietly southwards, skirting the graveyard. They were visible for a long time, and Theo kept looking back at Elliott and Janey. But finally Eve managed to turn his head, and Theo gazed towards the empty sky and clutched Eve, and together they rushed away to meet the future at last.

*

With the embers of the East Wing still coiling with smoke behind them, Janey faced Dad, Ben and Elliott. The sun was beginning to set.

'Do you need any help?' Dad said hesitantly to her. 'Practical support, I mean. I can help find you a place away from here, if that's what you want ...'

'Oh, I think I'll be all right,' Janey replied with a grin. 'I'm used to looking after myself.'

'There must be something we can do for you,' Ben said.

Janey smiled. 'Nothing. Truly there isn't. Not one thing. You've already given more than I could ever have believed. More than I should have asked for.'

Elliott leaned heavily on his left side. His knee still hurt. 'But what will you do?' he asked, worried for her. 'I mean, without the ghost children to keep you company? Won't you be lonely?'

Janey gave all three of them a smile that was as warm as strawberries in sunshine.

'Actually, I've made a few plans,' she confided. 'Nothing much, but there's something I've wanted to do for a long time. And, well, if you don't mind, I thought I might as well begin now . . .'

Janey's hand rose to Elliott's cheek. She left it there for a long time.

Then she turned away from Elliott, Ben and Dad and began to walk away across the western lawns.

A large expanse of grass stretched ahead of her.

Janey strode towards the graveyard. Reaching it, she touched four of the headstones. Soft mosses crumbled against her dry fingers.

In the distance the smoking ruins of the East Wing were still crackling with fire. Janey watched for a while. Then she bent towards a bush. Late-blooming roses poked through its leaves. Smiling, Janey fixed a red rose to a buttonhole in her dress. Then she glanced towards a mildewed wooden bench. It sat like a neglected, lonely thing at the southern end of the graveyard.

Walking across to the bench, Janey sat down. She reached into a pocket of her dress and took out a paperback book. Read a page or two. Slowly lowered the book again.

Stared around.

Peered in all directions.

The graveyard was entirely empty.

In the west, the sun started sinking below the horizon. It would be dark soon, but if she had no disruptions

Janey thought she might just have time to polish off the first couple of chapters, maybe more.

She brought the book back up to read. It was an excellent book. A racy thriller.

Crossing her knees, she became quite engrossed.

Nothing interrupted her.

Twenty minutes later, when Elliott checked from the kitchen window of Glebe House, Janey and her bench looked like a joined silhouette against a darkening sky.

Janey read and read.

When the natural light faded, she went back to her own house in the village. But she didn't stay there. She returned to the graveyard, snugly wrapped in a practical woollen jumper and carrying a flask of tea. She sat back down on the bench, placing the flask beside her.

She pulled the jumper over her narrow shoulders.

She switched on a bright torch.

It was a warm evening. A good evening for staying out late.

Long past midnight, when Elliott checked on her again, Janey was still reading happily.